MW00779004

WWW.MICHAELMCBRIDE.NET
MICHAEL MCBRIDE

amazon kindle

$2.99 AND UP

"MCBRIDE JUST KEEPS GETTING BETTER."
- HELLNOTES

"FULL-ON TERROR."
- HORROR WORLD

"...IMPRESSIVELY DARK, UTTERLY BLEAK..."
- TWILIGHT RIDGE

NO ONE LEAVES THE
RAINFOREST ALIVE

THE NEXT PHASE OF
EVOLUTION HAS ARRIVED

IF THE HEAT DOESN'T GET
YOU...THE COYOTE WILL

EXTINCTION IS ONLY
THE BEGINNING

HOW FAR WOULD YOU
GO TO SAVE YOUR CHILD?

5 NOVELLAS
1 MASSIVE VOLUME

WITHOUT CHAOS
NOTHING CAN EVOLVE

Also by Michael McBride

NOVELS

Ancient Enemy
Bloodletting
Burial Ground
Fearful Symmetry
Predatory Instinct
The Coyote
Vector Borne

NOVELLAS

F9
Remains
Snowblind
The Event

COLLECTIONS

Category V

MICHAEL McBRIDE

INNOCENTS LOST

A SUPERNATURAL THRILLER

FACTOR V MEDIA

Innocents Lost: A Supernatural Thriller copyright © 2011 by Michael McBride

All Rights Reserved.

This book is a work of fiction. Names, characters, places and incidents are either products of the author's imagination or used fictitiously. Any resemblance to actual events, locales, or persons, living or dead, is entirely coincidental. All rights reserved. No part of this publication may be reproduced or transmitted in any form or by any means, electronic or mechanical, without permission in writing from Michael McBride.

For more information about the author, please visit his website: www.michaelmcbride.net

For my grandparents

Special Thanks to Shane Staley, David Marty, and Steve Souza; Brian Keene; Leigh Haig; Zach McCain; Gene O'Neill; Jeff Strand; Bill Rasmussen; my amazing family; and, most importantly, all of my readers, without whom this book would not exist.

PROLOGUE

June 20th

Six Years Ago

I

Evergreen, Colorado

"Happy Birthday to yooouuu."

The song ended with laughter and applause.

"Make a wish, honey," Jessie said. She raised the camera and focused on the child who was her spitting image: chestnut hair streaked blonde by the sun, eyes the blue of the sky on the most perfect summer day, and a radiant smile that showed just a touch of the upper gums.

Savannah wore the dress she had picked out specifically for her party, black satin with an indigo iridescence that shifted with the light. She rose to her knees on the chair, leaned over the cake, and blew out the ring of ten candles.

The camera flashed and the group of girls surrounding her clapped again.

"What did you wish for?" Preston asked.

"You know I can't tell you, Dad. Sheesh."

"Why don't you girls run outside and play while I serve the cake and ice cream," Jessie said. "And after that we can open *presents.*"

"All right!" Savannah hopped out of the chair and merged into the herd of girls funneling out the back door into the yard. More laughter trailed in their wake.

Preston crossed the kitchen and closed the door behind them.

"So are all eight of them really spending the night here?" he asked, glancing out the window over the sink as he removed a stack of plates from the cupboard. The girls made a beeline toward the wooden jungle gym. One had already reached the ladder to the tree house portion and another slid down the slide.

"Do you really think the answer will change if you ask enough times, Phil?" She took the plates from her husband, set them on the table, and began to cut the cake. "Besides, they'll be sleeping in the family room with a pile of movies. The most we'll hear from down the hall is a few giggles. Could you grab the ice cream from the freezer?"

"So what you're saying is they'll be distracted." Preston eased up behind his wife, cupped her hips, and leaned into her.

She swatted his leg. "With a houseful of kids? Are you out of your mind?"

"I wasn't proposing they watch."

"Would you just get the ice—?"

The phone rang from the cradle on the wall.

Jessie elbowed him back, snatched the cordless handset, and answered while licking a dollop of frosting from her fingertip.

"Hello?"

Her smile vanished and her eyes ticked toward her husband.

"I'll take it in the study," Preston said. He removed the gallon of Rocky Road from the freezer, set it on the table, and hurried down the hallway.

"He'll be right there," Jessie said. Her voice faded behind him.

He ducked through the second doorway on the right and closed the door behind him. All trace of levity gone, he picked up the phone.

"Philip Preston," he answered.

"Please hold for Assistant Special Agent-in-Charge Moorehead," a female voice said. There was a click and then silence.

Preston paced behind his desk while he waited. He pulled back the curtains and looked out into the yard. Two of the girls twirled a jump rope on the patio for a third, while several others fired down the slide. Savannah and another girl arced back and forth on the swings. He couldn't believe his little girl was already ten years old. Where had the time gone? In a blink, she had gone from toddler to pre-teen. In less than that amount of time again, she would be off on her own, hopefully in college—

"Special Agent Preston," a deep voice said. He could tell by his superior's tone that something bad must have happened.

♦

Preston worked out of the Denver branch of the Federal Bureau of Investigation, thirty miles to the northeast of the bedroom community of Evergreen where he lived. The Lindbergh Law of 1932 gave the Crimes Against Children Division the jurisdiction to immediately investigate the disappearance of any child of "tender age," even before twenty-four hours passed and without the threat that state lines had been crossed. As a member of the Child Abduction Rapid Deployment, or CARD, team, he was summoned to crime scenes throughout the states of Colorado and Wyoming, often before the local police. It was a depressing detail that caused such deep sadness that by the time he returned home, even his soul ached. But it was an important job, and at least at the end of the day, unlike so many he encountered through the course of his work, his wife and daughter were waiting for him with smiles and kisses in the insulated world he had created for them.

"Yes, sir."

"Check your fax machine."

"Yes, sir." Preston allowed the curtains to fall closed and rounded his desk to where the fax machine sat on the corner. A stack of pages lay facedown on the tray. He grabbed them and took a seat in the leather chair, facing the computer. "Okay. I have it now. What am I—?"

His words died as he flipped through the pages. They were copies of slightly blurry photographs, snapped from a distance through a telescopic lens. Even though they were out of focus and the subjects partially obscured by the branches of a mugo pine hedge, he recognized them immediately.

"I don't get it," he whispered. "Where did these come from?"

"They arrived in the mail here at the Federal Building today. Plain white envelope. No return address. A handful of partial fingerprints we're comparing against the database now. We're tracking the serial numbers on the film to try to determine where they were processed."

There were a dozen pictures. One of him approaching a small white ranch-style house. Another of him standing on the porch, glancing back toward the street while he waited for the door to be answered. Several of him talking to a disheveled woman, Patricia Downey, mother of Tyson, who had disappeared five hours prior.

He didn't need to check the date stamp to know that these had been taken nearly three months ago in Pueblo, just over a hundred miles south of Denver. No suspects. Loving mother and doting father, neither of whom had brushed with the law over anything more severe than a speeding ticket. Middle class, decent neighborhood. And an eight year-old boy who had never made it home from the elementary school only three blocks away on a Thursday afternoon.

"This doesn't make sense," Preston said. "Why would anyone take these pictures, let alone mail them to us?"

He parted the blinds again and looked out upon the back yard. Nine girls still giggled and played. Savannah swung high, launched herself from the seat, and landed in a stumble. She barely paused before clambering back into the swing.

"Look at the last one," Moorehead said.

Preston's stomach dropped with those somber words. He shuffled past a series of pictures that showed him walking back to where he had parked at the curb after the hour-long interview with the Downeys.

"Jesus."

His heart rate accelerated and the room started to spin.

In one motion, he removed his Beretta from the recess in his desk drawer and jerked open the curtains again. Little girls still slid and jumped rope, but only one swing was occupied. The one upon which his daughter had been sitting only moments earlier swung lazily to a halt. As did the branches of the juniper shrubs behind the swing set.

"No, no, no!" he shouted.

The phone fell from his hand and clattered to the floor beside the faxed pages, the top image of which featured a snapshot of his house from across the street, centered upon Savannah as she removed a bundle of letters from the mailbox.

He ran down the hall and through the kitchen.

"Phil!" Jessie called after him. "What's going on?"

He burst through the back door and hit the lawn at a sprint, nearly barreling into one of the girls twirling the rope.

"Savannah!"

The activity around him slowed. Two of the girls stared down at him from the top of the slide, faces etched with fear. He ran to the girl on the swing, a dark-haired, pigtailed slip of a child, and took her by the shoulders.

"Where's Savannah?"

Startled, the girl could only shake her head.

Preston shoved away.

"Savannah!"

He shouldered through the hedge and hurdled the split-rail fence into the small field of wild grasses and clusters of scrub oak that separated the houses in this area of the subdivision.

"Savannah!"

A crunching sound behind him.

He whirled to see Jessie emerge from the junipers down the sightline of his pistol.

"What's wrong?" she screamed. "Where's Savannah?"

She must have read his expression, the panic, the sheer terror, and clapped her hands over her mouth.

Preston turned back to the field, tears streaming down his cheeks, trembling so badly he could barely force his legs to propel him deeper into the empty field toward the rows of fences and the gaps between them where paths led to the neighboring streets.

"Savannah!"

His voice echoed back at him.

He fell to his knees, rocked back, and bellowed up into the sky.

"Savannah!"

Chapter One

June 20th

Present Day

I

22 Miles West of Lander, Wyoming

"How much farther?" Lane Thomas asked. He swiped the sweat from his red face with the back of his hand.

Dr. Lester Grant had grown weary of the question miles ago. These graduate students were supposed to be the future of anthropology, and here they were braying like downtrodden mules.

"We're nearly there," Les said, comparing the printout of the digital photograph to the surrounding wilderness.

It was the summer session, so rounding up volunteers had been a chore, even though the opportunity to be published in one of the academic journals should have had them chomping at the bit. Granted, they had left the University of Wyoming in Laramie several hours before the sun had even thought about rising and driven for nearly three hours before they reached the end of the pavement and the rutted dirt road that wended up into the Wind River Range of the Rocky Mountains. Another hour of navigating switchbacks and crossing meadows where the road nearly disappeared entirely, and they reached the foot of the game trail that the hiker who had emailed him the photographs had said would be there. That was nearly two hours ago now. They'd taken half a dozen breaks already, and would be lucky if they'd managed to reach the three mile mark.

"Can we switch off again?" Jeremy Howard asked in a nasal, whiny tone. "Breck's making it so that I'm bearing all of the weight."

"Give me a break," the blonde, Breck Shaw, said. She hefted the handles of the crate they carried between them for emphasis, causing Jeremy to stumble.

"That's enough," Les snapped. They were adults, for God's sake. Sure, the crate containing the university's magnetometer was quite heavy, but they all had to pay their dues, as he once had himself.

They proceeded in silence marred by the crackle of detritus underfoot.

The path had faded to the point that it was nearly non-existent. At first, it had been choppy with the hoof prints of deer and elk, but after they had crossed over the first ridge and forded a creek, it had grown smooth. Knee-high grasses reclaimed it in the meadows. Only beneath the shelter of the ponderosa pines and the aspens, where the edges of the trail were lined with yellowed needles and dead leaves, was it clearly evident. How had that hiker found this path anyway? They were hundreds of miles from the nearest town with a population large enough to support a Wal-Mart Supercenter, and at an elevation where there was snow on the ground eight months out of the year. And this was so far out of the commonly accepted range of the Plains Indian Tribes, a generic title that encompassed the Arapahoe, Cheyenne, Crow, and Lakota, among others, that it made precious little sense for the site in the photographs to exist in the first place.

Which was what made the discovery so thrilling.

Les didn't realize how accustomed he'd grown to the constant chatter of starlings and finches until the sounds were gone. Only the wind whistled through the dense forestation, the pine needles swishing as the branches rubbed together. The ground was no longer spotted with big game and rodent scat. Patches of snow clung to the shadows at the bases of the towering pines and beneath the scrub oak, evidence of what he had begun to suspect. The air was indeed growing colder.

An unusual tree to the left of the path caught his attention. The trunk of the pine had grown in a strange corkscrew fashion, almost as though it had been planted by some omnipotent hand in a twisting motion. He fingered the pale green needles, which hung limply from branches that stood at obscene angles from the bizarre trunk.

"Can we take a quick break so I can get my coat out of my backpack?" Breck asked.

Les didn't reply. He was focused on an aspen tree several paces ahead. It too had an unusual spiral trunk. What could have caused them to grow in such a manner? He was just about to run his palm across its bark, which looked like it would crumble with the slightest touch, when he noticed the large mound of stones at the edge of the clearing ahead.

"We're here," he said.

He slipped out of his backpack and removed his digital camera.

"It's about time," Lane said. "I was starting to think we might have walked right past..."

Les's student's words were blown away by the wind as he walked past the first cairn and began snapping pictures. The clearing was roughly thirty yards in diameter. More corkscrewed trees grew at random intervals. They weren't packed together as tightly as those in the surrounding forest, but just close enough together to partially hide the constructs on the ground from the air. There were more mounds of stones in a circular pattern around the periphery of the clearing, all piled nearly five feet tall. He paused and performed a quick count. There were twenty-seven of them, plus a conspicuous gap where there was room for one more. Short walls of stacked rocks, perhaps a foot tall, led from each cairn to the center of the ring like the spokes of a wagon wheel. The earth between them was lumpy and uneven. Random tufts of buffalo grass grew where the sun managed to reach the dirt, which was otherwise barren, save for a scattering of pine needles.

"Why don't you guys start setting up the magnetometer," he called back over his shoulder as he stepped over the shin-high stack of stones that had been laid to form a complete circle just inside the twenty-seven cairns, and approached the heart of the creation.

At the point where the spokes met, more twisted trees surrounded a central cairn, which was wider and taller than the others. As he neared, Les could tell that it wasn't a solid mound at all, but a ring.

The formation of stones was a Type 6 Medicine Wheel like the one at Bighorn in the northern portion of the state, only on a much grander scale. Medicine wheels had been found throughout the Rocky Mountains from Wyoming all the way north into Alberta, Canada. They predated the modern Indian tribes of the area, which still used them for ceremonial rituals to this day. No one was quite certain who originally built them or for what purpose, only that they were considered sacred sites by the remaining Native American cultures, all of which had various myths to explain their creation. If this was a genuine medicine wheel, then it would be the southernmost discovered, and the most elaborate by far.

The emailed photographs had given him no reason to question its authenticity; however, now that he saw it in person, he was riddled with doubt. The stone formations were too well maintained. Not a single rock was out of place, nor had windblown dirt accumulated against the cairns to support an overgrowth of wild grasses. No lichen covered the stones, which, upon closer inspection, appeared to be granite. And the pictures had been taken in such a manner as to exclude the odd trunks.

Here he was, standing in the middle of what could prove to be the anthropological discovery of a lifetime, and he suddenly wished he'd never found this place. It was an irrational feeling, he knew, but there was just something…wrong with the scene around him.

He reached the center of the clearing and used the coiled trunk of a pine to propel himself up to the top of the ring of stones. The ground inside was recessed, the inner stones staggered in such a way as to create a series of steps. And at the bottom, in the dirt, saved from the wind, was a jumble of scuff marks preserved by time. The aura of coldness seemed to radiate from within it.

"Dr. Grant," Jeremy called from the tree line. "We need a little help setting up this machine."

"You're just trying to force that piece where it doesn't belong," Breck said.

"Then you do it, Little Miss Know-It-All."

Les sighed and climbed back down from what he had unconsciously begun to think of as a well, and headed back to join the group. For whatever reason, he dreaded assembling the magnetometer.

He suddenly feared what they would find.

II

Evergreen, Colorado

Preston sat in his forest-green Jeep Cherokee, staring across the street toward the dark house. He couldn't bring himself to go in there. Not today. But he couldn't force himself to leave yet either. Once upon a time, it had been his home, a place filled with love and laughter. Now it was a rotting husk, a shadow of its former self. The white paint had begun to peel where it met the trim, and there were gaps in the roof where shingles had blown away. The hedges in the yard had grown wild and unkempt, the lawn feral.

His life had ended in that house. The world had collapsed in upon itself and left him with nothing but pain.

And it had been all his fault.

His child, the light of his life, had been stolen from him because of his involvement in a case, and he still didn't know why. Over the last six years, he had begun to piece together a theory. Unfortunately, that's all it was. A theory. Grasping at straws was what his superiors had called it before his termination. Over the past year, nearly eight hundred thousand children were reported missing. While most were runaways, more than a third of them were abducted by family members or close friends. Many of these children resurfaced over the coming weeks, while still others never did. It was the smallest segment, the children who vanished at the apparent hands of strangers, that was the focus of his attention. At least privately. Professionally, he performed his job better than he ever had. After Savannah's abduction, he had thrown himself into it with reckless abandon, and at no small personal sacrifice. On a subconscious level, he supposed he hoped that by helping to return the missing children to their frightened parents that the universe might see fit to return his to him. But there was more to it than that. It was a personal quest, an obsession, and it had finally led him to a pattern.

Factoring out all of the kidnappings for ransom, the abductions by estranged parents or family friends, and the crimes of opportunity, where the child was simply in the wrong place at the wrong time, left Preston with a much smaller field to investigate. By narrowing his scope further to encompass only missing children from stable, two-parent, at least superficially loving homes, he winnowed the cases in his jurisdiction down to a handful each year. And of those, if he set the age range at Savannah's at the time of her disappearance, plus-or-minus three years, he was left with four cases annually over the past six and a half years. Not an average of four. Not three one year and five the next. Exactly four. And they were spread out by season. One child each year in the spring, another in the summer, a third in the fall, and a fourth in the winter. And all within two weeks of the four most important dates on the celestial calendar—the vernal and autumnal equinoxes, and the summer and winter solstices.

The kidnappings were the work of a single individual: The man who had stolen his daughter from him. The same man who had sent the photographs of him at the Downey house, who had been within fifty yards of him at a point in time when if Preston had known, he could have prevented the abduction of his cherished daughter, and the twenty-three children who came after her, with a single bullet.

Why could no one else see it? Why didn't they believe him?

Because he knew all too well that the parents of missing children would say or do anything if there was a chance of learning the fate of their son or daughter, even if it meant formulating a theory from a set of points that on paper appeared completely random, like forming constellations from the stars in the night sky.

Preston focused again on the house, but still couldn't bring himself to press the button on the garage door opener and pull the idling Cherokee inside. There was only solitude waiting for him within those walls, and the heartbreaking memories he was forced to endure with every breath he took. The house was a constant reminder of the greatest mistake of his life, but more than that, it was a beacon, the only location on the planet that Savannah had ever called her own. He still held out hope that wherever she was, one of these days she would simply appear from nowhere and return to her home. To him. It was the reason he would never allow himself to sell it. The one wish he allowed himself to pray would come true.

It was all he had.

He slid the gearshift into drive and headed south, pretending he didn't know exactly where he was going. Ten minutes later he was on the other side of town, parked in front of a Tudor-style two-story, upon which the forest encroached to the point of threatening to swallow it whole. Light shined through the blinds covering the windows. With a deep breath, he climbed out of the car and approached the porch.

The house positively radiated warmth, reminding him of what should have been. He pressed the doorbell and backed away from the door.

Shuffling sounds from the other side of the door, then a muffled voice.

"Just a second."

The door opened inward. A woman stood in the entryway, cradling a swaddled baby in the crook of her left arm. She brushed a strand of blonde bangs out of her eyes with the back of her right hand, which held a bottle still dripping from recently being heated in boiling water.

"Hi, Jessie," he said.

She still had the most amazing eyes he'd ever seen.

"Philip," she whispered. "You shouldn't be here."

"He's beautiful, Jess." He nodded to the baby. "How old is he by now?"

"Phil…"

They stood in an awkward silence for several long moments.

"You remember what today is?" Preston finally asked.

"Of course," she whispered. "Do you honestly think I could ever forget?"

He shook his head and looked across the lawn toward the forest.

"What happened to us, Jess?"

"I'm not getting into this with you again."

"Does he at least treat you well?"

"Who? Richard?" Anger flashed in her eyes. "He's emotionally stable, physically available, and isn't hell-bent on his own systematic destruction. And I don't cringe when he touches me. What more could a girl want?"

"But does he make you happy?"

She sighed. "Of course, Phil. I wouldn't have married him if he didn't." The baby started to cry, and quickly received the bottle. Jessie shuffled softly from one foot to the other in a practiced motion Preston remembered well. Only it had been with a different child, in a different lifetime entirely. "Why are you really here?"

"I needed to know that you were okay." He glanced back at her and offered a weak smile before looking away again. It was still impossible to think of her as anything other than the woman he had loved for the better part of his life, since the first time he had laid eyes on her. It hurt deep down to think of her as anything other than his wife. "That's all."

He had to turn away so she wouldn't see the shimmer of tears in his eyes, and used the momentum to spur his feet back toward his car.

"Phil."

He paused, blinked back the tears, and turned to face her again. Even with the recent addition of the wrinkles at the corners of her mouth and eyes, she was still the most stunning woman he had ever seen. And the baby seemed to make her glow. He couldn't bring himself to ask her his name.

"Are you all right?" she asked.

He shook his head, releasing streams of tears down his cheeks. No, he would never be all right ever again.

"Do you still blame me, Jessie?"

"You invited the danger into our home, whether intentionally or not," she whispered. "I will always blame you."

"So will I," he said, and struck off toward his car again. "I hope you have a good life, Jess. You deserve to be happy."

He heard her start to softly cry as she closed the door.

"Don't ever let him out of your sight," Preston said. "Ever."

His heart broke once more as he walked away from the love of his life.

III

22 Miles West of Lander, Wyoming

Les stood beside one of the cairns in the outer ring and watched his students perform their tasks as they had been taught. Jeremy guided the magnetometer in straight lines between the short walls that formed the spokes of the wagon wheel design. He wore the sensing device's harness over his shoulders and held the receptor, which looked like an industrial vacuum cleaner, a foot above the detritus. It interpreted the composition of the ground based on its magnetic content, and forwarded its readings into a program on Les's laptop that created a three-dimensional map of the earth to roughly ten meters in depth. Every type of rock had varying content of ferrous material and left a different magnetic signature, as did extinguished campfires, the foundations of prehistoric ruins, and various artifacts lost through the ages. Often, one ancient site was built upon another when a more modern culture eclipsed its forebear, like the Acropolis in Athens rose from the rubble of a Mycenaean megaron. If there was an older structure beneath this one, they would be able to find and map it without so much as brushing away the topsoil, but of greater importance were the relics left behind by the Native Americans who had meticulously crafted this ornate design. Hopefully, these buried clues would provide some indication of the function of the medicine wheel, the identity of its creators, and the reason it had been erected in the first place.

The magnetometer would also serve a secondary function he had chosen not to vocalize. Primitive societies often built cairns to mark the burial mounds of individuals of significance. If there were indeed corpses interred under their feet, then the magnetometer would reconstruct their unmistakable signals as well in hazy shades of gray. Fortunately, they had yet to isolate any remains. Based on the condition of the stones and the level of preservation, he feared any bodies they discovered might not be as ancient as he would prefer.

So far, the only signals had come from rocks under the soil, in no apparent pattern and of varying mineral content, save for one square object roughly a foot down, midway between where he stood now and the central ring of stones. Breck and Lane had cordoned off the square-yard above it with string and long metal tent pegs, and had begun to excavate in centimeter levels. They were only six inches down, and had yet to sift through anything more exciting than the coarse dirt.

"I still don't think this thing is working right," Jeremy said. "I can't seem to get rid of that strange, streaky feedback a couple yards down."

"I told you that you were putting it together wrong," Breck said.

"You could always switch with me and lug this thing around, princess."

Les rolled his eyes and tuned them out. Their bickering was grating on his nerves. Besides, he needed to try to sort out his thoughts, to figure out exactly what was so wrong with this site.

"There's another one over here!" Jeremy called. "Same size, same shape, and same location within this section."

"Mark it and try the next section over," Les said. Two could be a coincidence. Three was a pattern. "Let me know immediately if it's there."

What was roughly five inches square, half an inch thick, and crafted from metal? He would know soon enough, he supposed, but the objects made him nervous. The Bighorn Medicine Wheel predated the development of Native American metallurgical skills. If what they uncovered was manmade, then this site wasn't nearly as old as it had been designed to appear.

The wind shifted, bringing with it a scent that crinkled his nose. It smelled like something had crawled off into the forest to die. He stepped around the cairn and walked into the wind, but the smell dissipated. A cursory inspection of the forest's edge didn't reveal the carcass he had expected to find. Perhaps the detritus had already accumulated over it. The breeze waned, and he returned to his post, where he resumed his supervisory duties.

"Right here," Jeremy said. "Just like the other two. What do you want me to do?"

"For now, just mark it and keep going with the magnetometer. I want to map as much of the site as we can before sundown."

"I could just dig it up really quickly."

"That's not how it works and you know it."

Les sighed. The impatience of youth.

"Can't blame a guy for trying," Jeremy said with a shrug, and went back to work.

Another gust of wind brought the stench back to Les. The breeze made a whistling sound as it passed through the stacked stones of the cairn.

He crept closer and the smell intensified. The source of the vile reek was definitely somewhere under the cairn. He leaned right up against it and tried to peer through the tiny gaps between the stones. At first, he saw only shadows, so he crouched and inspected the lower portion, nearer the ground. He gagged and covered his mouth and nose with his dirty hand.

There was a dark recess behind the stacked rocks. He could barely discern a smooth section of something the color of rust. A rounded segment of bone through which thin sutures coursed. Just the barest glimpse and he knew exactly what was entombed within those stones.

"We've reached the artifact," Breck called. "What do you want us to do?"

Les couldn't find the voice to answer. He craned his neck to see through another gap below the last. An eye socket in profile, the sharp stub of the nasal bones, crusted with a coating of dirt and blood.

A spider scurried over the cheekbone and disappeared into a small fissure in the ridged maxilla above a row of tiny teeth.

There was no doubt it was human. And it definitely wasn't thousands of years old.

His legs gave out and deposited him on his rear end in the dirt. He scanned the forest, expecting to find whoever had done this watching him from the shadows.

"Dr. Grant? What you want us to do with this?"

He whirled in her direction. These kids were his responsibility. He needed to get them out of here this very second.

Breck raised her eyebrows to reiterate the question. She and Lane knelt over the square hole in the earth, mounds of dirt to either side by the screens they had used to sift through them. They must have recognized something in his expression, for both of them backed slowly away from him.

"Gather your belongings," Les snapped.

"What about the magnetometer?" Jeremy asked.

"Leave it!"

Les crawled away from the cairn and shoved to his feet. He grabbed his backpack and strode toward where Breck and Lane cringed. Fear shimmered in their eyes.

"Get your backpacks. Hurry up!"

"But Dr. Grant—" Lane started.

"We don't have time for this!"

The graduate students scurried away from their excavation. Les heard a shuffling sound as they donned their gear. He knelt by the hole and stared into its depths.

A tin with rounded edges peeked out of the ground. He brushed away the loose dirt to reveal three rows of numbers and letters that had been crudely scratched into the metal.

19
3-20
V.E.

He pulled one of the tent pegs from the cordon and pried at the corner of the object.

The top portion of the tin popped open to reveal its contents.

A DVD-R in an ordinary plastic jewel case. The same series of numbers and letters had been scrawled on the disk in black marker.

The case was smeared with blood.

IV

Evergreen, Colorado

Preston sat on the back porch in a folding lawn chair, watching night approach from the eastern horizon over the jagged crests of the distant foothills as he did whenever he had the opportunity. He prayed that one of these evenings, a young woman would simply emerge from the twilight and step through the overgrown juniper hedge and back into his life. Would she still recognize him? Six years was a long time to a child, but he would devote his remaining days to reminding her if she didn't.

He drew a swig from the bottle of Bud and set it back in his lap. It was all he could do to resist the urge to drink himself into a stupor, as if that wasn't exactly how he had stumbled through the last six years.

The odds were stacked against him. With each hour that passed following an abduction, the chances of the child returning home diminished exponentially. After so many years, there were really only two viable outcomes: Either Savannah was somewhere far from home and would never come back, or she was dead. Both meant he would never see his child again, never know what happened to her. But he couldn't allow himself to abandon all hope or he'd be tasting the oil from the barrel of his pistol. And then what would happen if by some miracle his daughter finally did find her way back? Someone needed to man the lighthouse, and if he didn't, who would? Jessie had already moved on, but he knew he would never be able to. Not until Savannah appeared again...or they discovered her body.

He sobbed at the thought, leapt to his feet, and hurled the bottle across the yard. It struck the tree house at the top of the slide and shattered. Foam slid down the weathered wood and glass shards fell into the sun-fried grass. The chains on the swings had rusted long ago, and the branches of the cottonwood had grown around the whole construct.

The back door of his neighbor's house opened and he heard tentative footsteps on the wooden deck beyond the fence. They all knew better by now than to ask him if he was okay. Besides, it wasn't the first bottle he had broken in the yard, as evidenced by the fragments in the dead lawn that reflected the red of the setting sun behind him. After a long pause, the neighbor's door closed softly and Preston was alone again.

He watched the first star twinkle into being and made the same wish he always made, then righted the chair he had toppled in his hurry to vent his anger. He turned toward the open door to the kitchen, obviously in need of another beer.

Movement caught his attention from the corner of his eye, a rustle of branches, a shift in the lengthening shadows.

He spun to face the yard again.

A dark face.

The whites of eyes.

Juniper branches shook and he heard the crunch of invisible tread.

Drawing his Beretta from the holster under his left arm, Preston sprinted toward the shrubs, swatting branches away from his face as he barreled through. He exploded from the far side and leaped over the fence into the closely-cropped field. Rear porch lights turned the fences to silhouettes in the distance. The clusters of scrub oak cast long shadows.

"Freeze!" Preston shouted. He swept his pistol from one side of the clearing to the other as his voice echoed away into oblivion.

A dog barked, and several more joined the raucous chorus.

Dark shapes appeared in windows before vanishing again.

A stooped old man hobbled slowly across the mouth of the path on the sidewalk of the street beyond.

Only the leaves fluttered on the breeze.

Nothing else moved.

Preston's shoulders slumped and his arms fell to his sides.

He was certain he had seen someone, if only for a split-second.

Holstering his weapon, he walked deeper into the clearing to beat the bushes and confirm what his eyes already insisted.

There was no one else out there.

V

22 Miles West of Lander, Wyoming

They had called nine-one-one the moment the first cell phone picked up a signal. A police officer had been waiting at the base of the trail when they arrived.

Les Grant now sat in the passenger seat of a Fremont County Sheriff's Department Blazer at the foot of the trailhead, his laptop open on his thighs. A matching SUV idled next to him. Two Lander Police Department cruisers were parked behind him to block off access to the road, cherries twirling, staining the night in alternating shades of red and blue. A white van stenciled with the letters ERT barred access to the path. The Emergency Response Team had already unloaded a handful of forensics techs, their packs brimming with gear to collect evidence. His Subaru Forester had been temporarily impounded while experts sifted through every last microscopic fiber in search of anything incriminating. He supposed he should have been angry, but he knew they would find nothing and return it to him in short measure. At least after taking statements from his students, who all showed various signs of shock, one of the policemen had driven them down the mountain to the nearest hospital for a full medical examination. First thing in the morning, Les would call the university and arrange for their transportation back to Laramie.

Considering he was the one who had brought them all here, and it was he who discovered the remains entombed in the cairn, the authorities had requested his continued presence until whatever questions arose were answered to their satisfaction. He felt as though he'd been sequestered to this car for hours already.

The initial email containing the pictures of the site had been sent to a general university email address, and from there routed to the College of Arts and Sciences, then to the Anthropology Department, before finally finding its way into his personal account. The brain trust at the Rocky Mountain Regional Computer Forensics Laboratory was already hard at work following the cyber-trail, but so far had been unable to produce more than an IP address that corresponded to a public internet terminal at the Laramie County Library in Cheyenne.

Whoever had sent it had wanted this site to be found, and by someone other than the police first, someone with enough anthropological knowledge to recognize the medicine wheel and its potential significance. He couldn't help but wonder why. And more importantly, why *him*, or had he simply been the unlucky recipient?

He watched the congregation of law enforcement officers gathered around the hood of the adjacent Blazer through the window. They pored over a series of maps detailing everything from elevation to the most recent satellite images while they gave the ERT crew a head start to gather whatever evidence they might be able to find before the entire circus descended upon the medicine wheel.

While he waited, Les used the time to seek answers to the questions that gnawed at the back of his mind.

He resumed his internet search. Thus far, he had only been able to confirm what he already knew. There were more than seventy documented medicine wheels throughout Montana, South Dakota, Wyoming, and the Canadian provinces of Saskatchewan and Alberta, which contained the greatest concentration. They were designed as "horizon calendars" to monitor and predict specific celestial events that coincided with important days of the year. Most had twenty-eight spokes to correspond with the lunar calendar. The cairns were placed in such a way that when looking from one to another at various points across the circle, certain stars would rise on the appropriate dates. He had never studied petroform astronomy in any depth, but he did understand the concept of using stars to chart the solstice. The helical rising of the star Fomalhaut signaled the commencement of a twenty-eight day countdown to the summer solstice, toward the end of which

Aldebaran would rise, two days prior to the event. Rigel would rise twenty-eight days after that, and Sirius another four weeks later to mark the end of summer. Other cairns would be aligned to provide a direct line of sight into the rising and setting sun on the day of the solstice. Was it possible that this medicine wheel had been built to the precise standards Native Americans had used eight hundred years ago? If so, Aldebaran already made its debut on the horizon last night. And what did the skeletal remains and the DVDs have to do with anything? Obviously, such recording devices were unavailable so many years ago, and although the more ancient medicine wheels had similar cairns, there was no historical record of the discovery of corpses inside of them.

And there was something else troubling him. The trees. What could have caused the pines and aspens in the immediate vicinity of the clearing to grow in a corkscrew fashion? There was a species of willow that commonly grew in a spiral manner, but very little regarding the mutation in other indigenous species. Similar groves had been discovered in Saskatchewan, northwest of the town of Hafford, which, coincidentally, was not far from the location of a smaller medicine wheel. Other instances were reported outside of Sedona, Arizona, where the odd growth patterns were attributed to mystical energy vortices that drew thousands of pilgrims every year. These spiraling vortices were claimed to induce a preternatural sense of well-being and feelings of rejuvenation in anyone who stood within range. It smacked of New Age mumbo-jumbo to Les.

A knock on the window startled him from his research.

He looked up to see the broad-shouldered, crew-cut Sheriff with the granite jaw that had ushered him into the vehicle. Dandridge, if he remembered correctly.

Les closed his laptop, tucked it under his arm, and opened the door. He stepped down from the passenger seat into a small crowd. He'd already been introduced to Lander Police Officers Carnahan and Wilcox with their blue uniforms during the first wave of interrogations, and Fremont County Sheriff's Department Deputies Henson and Miller in their matching brown jackets during the second.

"Deputy Henson will be taking you down to Lander, where we've arranged for accommodations in a motel for you and your students," Dandridge said.

The expression of disappointment on the deputy's face suggested he'd drawn the short straw.

"And from there?" Les asked.

"Once we've examined the crime scene and you've answered whatever questions we might come up with, you will be free to leave," Dandridge said. And as an afterthought, "We do apologize for the inconvenience."

"Come with me, Dr. Grant," Henson said. The deputy guided Les by the elbow toward the waiting cruiser.

Henson paused in front of the two doors on the passenger side, a moment of indecision that spoke volumes about how the authorities perceived Les, before finally opening the front door and ushering him inside.

He watched through the front windshield in the red and blue glare as the remaining four men started up the path into the wilderness. Tires kicked gravel up against the undercarriage as they began the return trip to civilization.

The impromptu parking lot at the base of the path fell away behind him in the side mirror, but Les couldn't shake the feeling that this wouldn't be the last time he saw this section of the forest.

VI

Evergreen, Colorado

Preston rolled over onto his back and stared up at the ceiling. A swatch of moonlight stretched across the angled ceiling from the gap above the curtains, creating an elongated X-shaped shadow from the ceiling fan, which turned slowly at the urging of a gentle breeze only it could feel. He had collapsed fully clothed on top of the bedspread several hours earlier, and while he was physically spent, his mind was far from exhausted. No matter how hard he tried, there would be no respite of sleep for him this night. After all, if his theory was correct, the man who had taken his daughter only had one night left to strike again before the summer solstice.

He thought about the intruder he was certain he had seen in his yard. Was it possible it was the same man he had been chasing for the last six years? And if so, why had the man chosen to reveal himself to Preston at this juncture? And where had he gone? There was no way that old guy could have sprinted across the field in the time it had taken him to pass through the juniper hedge. So where in the world had the man been hiding? Or, as Preston was reticent to contemplate, had he even truly been there at all? There had been no footprints or other signs of trespass to warrant calling for further investigation, and even if he had called it in, without any kind of empirical evidence, they would have dismissed his claims out-of-hand. Especially today.

With a sigh, he flopped over onto his side and faced the clock. 11:57 p.m. He wanted nothing more than for this day to finally end. However, the prospect of facing another year like the previous six made him sick to his stomach.

The time changed to 11:58.

He crawled over the edge of the bed and headed out of the bedroom he had shared with his wife, down the hallway, and into the kitchen, where the Maalox waited. After several gulps straight from the bottle, he opened the refrigerator. It contained only the remnants of a twelve-pack of Budweiser and take-out containers filled with partially consumed meals, fuzzy with mold. The last thing he needed right now was to further aggravate his digestive system.

His thoughts turned to the Beretta holstered on his nightstand. How easy would it be to simply open his mouth, press the barrel against his hard palate, and end his suffering?

"No," he said out loud, the sound of the lone word startling him in the silence. That bullet was reserved for the man who had ruined his life. Even if it took the rest of his days, he would see the look in the man's eyes when he jammed the barrel between them. He didn't need to make the man beg, nor did he care about repentance. He merely wanted to see a spark of recognition before he committed that micro-momentary expression of pain to memory. Only when that mental image grew stale would he turn his pistol upon himself. Until then, he would continue to dog the bastard's steps, regardless of the physical and emotional toll his obsession exacted.

He returned to the cupboard, pulled out the Maalox, and set it beside his laptop on the kitchen table.

"Breakfast of champions," he said as he sat down at the table and guzzled from the blue plastic container.

He opened his computer and the screen bloomed to life. His personal case file, which contained everything he could find on his daughter's abductor, both factual and speculative, was waiting for him. If there was a pattern to the kidnappings, then there had to be a way to predict them. He was just too blind to see it. Twenty-seven children, all of whom fit the same profile, had been stolen from their families in just under seven years, their disappearances equally spaced to correspond with celestial events, and within the coming day, he was sure there would be a twenty-eighth. The first had been an eleven year-old girl named, Sarah Schmaltz. He revisited her file for the thousandth time. What was special about her that had helped to trigger this chain of events? Why hadn't there been any missing children's cases that fit this particular *modus operandi* before her? She was an average-looking child from a middle-class upbringing in Fort Collins, Colorado. As far as he could tell, there was nothing extraordinary about her, but there had to be something he was overlooking, something—

His laptop chimed. An envelope icon appeared in the bottom corner of the screen, signaling the arrival of a new email.

The clock on the microwave read midnight on the nose.

Preston brushed the cursor, aligned the arrow with the envelope, and double-clicked the icon.

His inbox opened and downloaded the new message. Part of him expected—or maybe just hoped—that it would be from Jessie. Instead, the sender's name matched his own: Philip Preston. A right-click confirmed the email had originated from his own personal email account, quite possibly from this very laptop. Inside his home. The subject line read simply *Twenty-eight*.

He clicked his Sent Items folder, and confirmed that the email had indeed been composed within this very account at 10:03 p.m. and sent using the time-delay function to arrive at midnight.

A tiny paperclip icon indicated there was an attachment.

"Son of a bitch," he whispered.

His hands trembled as he opened the email.

He glanced again at the sender's name, and then at the keyboard over which his fingers were poised like the legs of twin spiders. Had whoever sent the message been sitting right here in this very spot as he did now? He hadn't heard the slightest sound, and he had only been fifteen feet away.

The body of the email was composed of three rows of numbers and letters:

28

6-21

S.S.

And below them was a picture of a darkened room. The faint reflection on the glass indicated it had been taken through a window at night. There was a bed against the far wall, and curled under a tangle of blankets, a small child slept, long blonde bangs crossing her peacefully slumbering features.

Chapter Two

June 21st

I

22 Miles West of Lander, Wyoming

Fremont County Sheriff Keith Dandridge surveyed the site from the edge of the forest. The scene before him was beyond his worst nightmares. In his eleven years in law enforcement, he had been involved in some of the most ghastly cases in the Rocky Mountain region, most notably the Schoolhouse Slaughter in Pine Springs eight years ago. A disgruntled, bipolar teacher named Irving Jepperson had lined up his class of twelve sixth grade students at the front of the room and fired upon them at close range with a shotgun. Four of the children had managed to escape through the window while the custodian and another teacher subdued him. Eight eleven and twelve year olds had been heaped on the floor at the foot of a chalkboard peppered with buckshot and spattered with blood, bone fragments, and gray matter when he arrived. There had been nothing left of their faces or upper torsos, leaving the parents to identify their children by their blood-soaked clothing and shoes. And somehow, even that carnage paled by comparison to the horror that unfolded before him now, perhaps not in sheer ferocity, but in the palpable evil that emanated from the clearing.

The amount of planning that had been invested into the creation of this tableau was staggering.

A ring of halogen lights encircled the wagon wheel design. They provided precious little illumination, and instead cast long shadows from the rock cairns and walls. More lights would have to be airlifted in with a supply of portable generators, but not until they had thoroughly scoured the ground for evidence. They couldn't afford for the rotors of a chopper to blow away even a single footprint, and the nearest other suitable landing area was a mile and a half to the northeast. For now, the ERT crew was gathering whatever they could find and photographing even the smallest stone from every appreciable angle.

With such an elaborate setup, Dandridge knew they would only discover what the killer wanted them to find. This was no haphazard burial site. An inordinate amount of time and care had gone into designing something meant to be seen.

This promised to be the longest night of his life.

"You're going to want to see this," an evidence tech he recognized as Brad Stewart said from his left, where two large piles of stones had been removed from one of the cairns and stacked to either side of it, framing a maw of shadows.

Dandridge reluctantly approached, accepted the proffered flashlight from Stewart, and shined it into the hollow base of the cairn.

"At a guess," Stewart said, "I'd wager she was killed roughly two years ago, but we'll have to wait for the ME for a more official assessment."

"She?"

"That's our working assumption. She's still too young and skeletally immature to tell definitively."

Dandridge crouched and had to cover the lower portion of his face with his handkerchief to combat the stench.

A handful of flies buzzed lazily at the periphery of the light's reach.

"For the love of God," Deputy Miller said from behind him. There was a crashing sound in the underbrush, then a retching noise as Miller was absolved of his dinner.

Dandridge studied the recess with the flashlight. A fully-articulated skeleton had been posed to face the center of the medicine wheel. Its palms had been drawn together and placed against the left side of its skull, its head canted slightly toward them in a twisted mockery of a peacefully sleeping child. There was a depressed fracture slightly anterior to the coronal suture, from which a spider web of cracks expanded. And based upon the size of the bones and the presence of the epiphyseal growth plate lines, he estimated she couldn't have been more than twelve years old. Rusted lengths of barbed wire had been wound around and through the skeleton to hold the remains in place. Tangles of hair and tattered skin still adorned the barbs. Clumps of blackened flesh clung to the bones at random intervals, while the rest had turned the color of rust and were crusted with flaking scales of dried blood. Frayed tendons had retracted and pulled away from their moorings, where the gristle of muscle attachments reminded him of the nubs at the ends of gnawed drumsticks. The cartilaginous joints were ebon and rotted, yet somehow managed to hold the appendages together. Flies crawled on the dirt, which was slimy and lumpy with the foul dissolution of the tissues that had sloughed from the body as it decomposed.

"All of the teeth are still intact," Dandridge said, sweeping the beam across the small face. "It shouldn't take long to provide a positive ID from dental records."

"If we're right, it might be even easier than that," Stewart said. "We were waiting for you before we watched the disks. There are tins buried halfway between the central and outer cairns, just like the professor said. We're still carefully digging them out of the ground. So far, the sampling we've loaded all confirm the presence of a video file in the neighborhood of half a gigabyte."

"How long is that?"

"Depending upon resolution, somewhere between twenty and forty minutes."

"And you haven't watched them yet?"

"We took samples of the blood smears and dusted for prints, but no, we saved that honor just for you."

Dandridge glanced at the remains one final time. He only hoped she hadn't suffered too badly. His gut, however, insisted otherwise.

"We have the disk that corresponds with this cairn loaded and waiting on a laptop," Stewart said. He paused. "Are you ready to do this?"

Dandridge nodded and rose to his feet. The last thing in the world he wanted to do right now was watch that infernal disk. He already had a pretty good idea of what it contained.

Stewart nodded toward the nearest overhead light, which had been mounted in the upper reaches of one of those sickly pines. An evidence tech he hadn't worked with before sat on a level portion of the twisted trunk, computer in his lap, a stack of tins in plastic evidence bags to his right. He looked up when Dandridge approached, quickly stood, and handed over the laptop. Dandridge sat on the tech's former perch and the others gathered around to watch. The tech offered one of the bagged tins from the pile, upon which several numbers and letters had been scratched.

"We suspect the top number is the victim's chronological order," the tech said. "The numbers below it are the month and day. No year. And there's still some debate, but I'm pretty sure the letters on the bottom line are abbreviations for vernal and autumnal equinox, and summer and winter solstice."

"How do I make this thing play?" Dandridge asked.

"It's already primed. You just have to double-click the file name."

Ordinarily, this was where the tech would not-so-discreetly mock his inferior technical skills, but tonight, no one envied him the task at hand.

Dandridge did as he was instructed and the media player opened. After a moment, a gray rectangle with a control bar beneath it appeared.

He drew a deep breath to steady his nerves, aligned the cursor with the PLAY button, and tapped the mouse.

The video began to roll.

II

Evergreen, Colorado

Preston imported the photograph into his image enhancement program and magnified it to the limits of its resolution, searching for anything that might provide a clue to the child's location. A bookcase next to the bed displayed the spines of young adult novels without any library stickers or other distinguishable markings. The poster beside it was of the Jonas Brothers, another of Hannah Montana was cropped at the edge of the picture by the pink curtains drawn back from the window. Either a night light or a digital clock produced a weak glow from the opposite side. The comforter was a uniform peach color and the bed appeared to be a standard-issue single. With her eyes closed and her bangs obscuring her features, he couldn't ascertain a single identifiable characteristic beyond hair color, and whatever subtle hue existed was attenuated by darkness.

"There has to be something here," he said. Why else would it have been sent to him before the fact? He had already checked the wire, and there had been no abductions within the last twenty-four hours, nor had any of the recent victims matched the pathetic description he had been able to generate: Caucasian female; blonde hair; approximate age of ten to twelve years old; eye color, height, and weight all indeterminate.

He sharpened the contrast and scooted back from the screen. The photograph had been taken from roughly two feet away from the window, and at an angle in order to peer around the partially-drawn drapes. Further manipulation of contrast and resolution allowed him to scrutinize the reflection on the glass from what appeared to be a streetlamp behind the photographer. He could clearly see the reflection of the camera, and the dark silhouette of the man holding it to his face: slumped shoulders, unkempt hair above a long face, ears with sagging lobes. No other details were readily apparent, as though the man existed in a perpetual state of shadow.

Preston could see the cut of the asphalt as a vague reflection, the hint of green from the lawn on the opposite side of the street at the foot of a dark, ranch-style house with a sedan parked in the driveway. It could have been any street in any neighborhood. He studied the periphery of the image. To one side, the reflection of a purple crabapple tree with white blossoms. To the other, a deciduous hedgerow.

"Damn it!" he shouted, knocking over the chair in his hurry to stand.

He had to be missing something.

After pacing the kitchen with his palms pressed against his forehead for several minutes, he righted the chair and sat in front of the monitor once again. He zoomed in as tightly as he could on the reflection of the house across the street, a ghost of an image through which he could see the outline of the small girl's shoulder under the bundle of blankets. There was no address on the house or the mailbox, at least that he could see. He focused on the car parked in the driveway, a newer model Saturn. More magnification distorted the vehicle, but allowed him to zoom in on the rear of the sedan and its license plate. The design was blurry, but he had seen it enough times to know which state had issued it. Two numbers to the left, what looked like a one above a zero, the trademark cowboy on the back of a bucking bronco beside it, and a combination of four numbers and letters to the right, none of which were legible thanks to the unfortunate alignment with the hedge.

A partial plate on a common model of car wouldn't get him far. However, Wyoming wasn't so overpopulated that license plates were assigned at random. The numbers on the left side indicated the county in which the vehicle was registered. A quick search confirmed that the number ten corresponded with Fremont County. Granted, there was no guarantee that the car wasn't parked in front of a house in a different county or state entirely, but it was all he had to go on, and if he left right this very moment, he could be there before sunrise.

Preston folded the laptop closed, tucked it under his arm, and sprinted toward his bedroom. He grabbed his keys and his sidearm from the nightstand and hurried to the garage. The Cherokee's tires screamed on the concrete as the car rocketed backward into the street. He slammed the brakes, punched it into gear, and raced toward the highway.

He was never going to make it in time. The abductor had a lead of several hours and knew exactly where he was going. All Preston had was a sparsely populated county filled with dozens of towns divided by mountainous topography. The largest city and county seat, Lander, seemed like the safest place to start, but what did he propose, cruising the streets one at a time until he found the house he had seen only in reflection? It didn't matter now. The first order of business was to alert the local authorities and see if he could call in a personal favor from someone in his unit at the FBI. He still had a long drive ahead of him, and mobilizing the locals to increase their patrols in any number of towns in a county spread out over nine thousand square miles based on a partial plate lifted from the image of a sleeping child when no crime had yet been committed was going to be a hard sell.

He snapped open his cell phone and began making the calls.

They were never going to find this little girl in time.

Unfortunately, he feared, that was the whole point.

III

22 Miles West of Lander, Wyoming

Sheriff Dandridge realized he was holding his breath and had to force himself to breathe. The video began with a clattering sound and perfect blackness marred by soft whimpering. He heard the scrape of footsteps before a single overhead bulb hanging from a cord bloomed with a snap, casting a weak bronze glare over a small room with cinder block walls. Cobwebs swayed in the upper left corner where they connected the rotting wooden joists above. With a rustling noise, the camera lowered and centered upon a workbench made of particle board, the surface scarred with cuts and gouges, and coated with a black crust. The floor beneath it was bare, packed earth or stone.

"Do any of you recognize this place?" Dandridge asked.

The others answered with shakes of their heads as though they had all lost their voices at once.

Dandridge returned his attention to the monitor. The whimpering grew louder and metamorphosed into shrill, panicked shrieks. A scuffing sound off screen, and a dark form eclipsed the view. The screams grew louder until they became a squeal of feedback. A man's back resolved in the center, the glare turning him to a silhouette of darkness, shoulders slumped, arms straining against the flailing body he held down on the workbench. After several unendurable minutes, the shadowed man stepped away and the camera focused on a young girl. She was bound to the table by thick, frayed ropes that stretched her arms and legs toward the four corners. Her dark hair was tangled and matted, her naked body smeared with dirt and blood. She bucked and screamed, then fell perfectly still. Her eyes widened and she shook her head violently from side to side, releasing a rush of blood from her nose.

"Please," she sobbed. "Please. No. I'll be good. I promise. I...I won't tell anyone."

Footsteps scuffed to her right and she turned in that direction. Her cheekbone was bruised, and a scabbed laceration ran through the crusted hair above her left ear.

A man's voice gently shushed her.

"I...I can't watch this," Miller said, shrinking away from the group.

Dandridge only wished he could do the same, for they all knew what was about to happen. The evidence was bound in barbed wire across the clearing.

The girl shook her head again and repeated the word "no" over and over. A metal cart rolled into view with a clatter. Rusted surgical implements from a bygone era were spread out evenly on a bloodstained towel.

"Mommy!" she screamed. "I want my mom! Please. Let me go. I need to go home!"

A green blur suddenly filled the screen. The lens focused on a poorly erased chalkboard upon which the same series of numbers and letters that adorned the disk and its case had been scrawled. In the room beyond, the child's pleas turned to screams. The chalkboard jittered before being jerked away from the camera.

A shadow crossed over the supine girl's body and the recorder zoomed in on the frightened child's face and torso. She was so young, her cheeks still chubby, what little skin showed through the filth smooth and porcelain. The shadow shifted and there was the sound of metal against metal.

The girl screamed and thrashed.

Again, there was a shushing sound, which only served to increase her exertions.

A pointed shadow traced the slope of her neck down to her jugular notch before the tip of a scalpel appeared, followed by a hand, the wrinkles in the knuckles lined with dried blood. The man pressed the blade into the skin, which dimpled and then parted with a swell of dark blood.

The child's cries were so filled with terror and pain that Dandridge found himself praying for them to end.

She trembled as the scalpel drew a line down the center of her narrow chest, then bucked so hard she nearly buried the blade in her upper abdomen.

The man made a growling sound and pulled the scalpel away. There was a crash as he slammed it onto the tray of utensils.

Ribbons of blood trickled to either side of the incision when she arched against her restraints in an effort to seize the momentary opportunity. She screamed for her mother and father, for help, for the pain to stop, until a large hand closed over her mouth and nose, and held her face still. Her muffled screams faded to whimpers and her eyes opened impossibly wide, the irises shivering.

A hammer struck her hairline from the top of the screen with a sickening crack, then disappeared again, trailing a tangle of hair. Blood pooled in the depression in her frontal bone where the skin had torn. She fell abruptly silent, her body motionless.

"Oh, God," Dandridge whispered. The laptop suddenly felt as though it was on fire, burning his legs, and he wanted nothing more than to hurl it to the ground. He had never seen anything so horrible in his life.

The girl's eyes glazed over and her lids slowly began to close.

After a moment's hesitation, the man loosened his grip and removed his hand from her face. Her lips had split under the pressure, smearing her entire mouth with blood.

"I don't think...I can't watch this," one of the officers said from behind Dandridge, then scampered away to vomit in the forest.

The child's chest rose and fell, subtly, slowly.

Dandridge had to look away, but only saw the girl's remains kneeling at the point where the cairn had been removed from above her.

He glanced back down at the monitor in time to see the hand return with the scalpel, which slid back into the incision past the depth of the blade.

Her only response was a sudden gasp and a flutter of her eyelids.

Dandridge forced himself to watch through tear-blurred eyes as warmth drained down his cheeks. He needed to know this monster, needed to understand him. For when the time arrived, and he swore it would, he was going to find this man, and he was going to kill him.

On the screen, the little girl was peeled apart, one strap of flesh, one muscle, one silvery tendon at a time in a careful and practiced display of vivisection skills until there wasn't enough blood left in her body to pump through her heart and the deep skeletal muscles shimmered wetly.

By the time the video ended, Dandridge sat alone, his body numb, his stomach roiling.

He surveyed the clearing, and through the assortment of twisted pines and aspens, counted twenty-six other lives similarly ended. And he was going to have to endure the videographies of their final moments.

Then he was going to hunt this man down, and he was going to rid the world of a scourge the likes of which it had never known before.

But first he needed to track down the satellite phone they carried for use in the remote areas of the county. It was imperative that he call his wife and physically make her check on their daughter. He couldn't imagine what would become of him if his beautiful child ended up on a film like this one.

No child should be subjected to such a violation of the body and soul.

IV

24 Miles North-northwest of Rawlins, Wyoming

Preston spiked his cell phone against the dashboard in frustration. He immediately regretted the decision and fished it from the floorboard to make sure it still worked. Anger seethed inside of him, but unfortunately, the scenario had played out just as he had expected. Without evidence of a crime, his department had been unable to act. He had heard the disbelief in his superior's voice after waking him from a sound sleep. Randall Washington was the new Assistant Special Agent-in-Charge. There was no history between them as there had been with M. Stephen Moorehead before his promotion, who might at least have humored him based on a photograph that he appeared to have sent himself. Washington, on the other hand, made no secret of his suspicions that Preston flirted with a breakdown, and that the pattern he discovered was circumstantial at best. His superior was disinclined to buy into the notion of a serial abductor in this day and age who planned his crimes to coincide with the pagan celestial calendar. While Preston didn't necessarily blame the Bureau for its doubts, tonight he needed its help for the sake of a child, and it had forsaken him.

The Fremont County Sheriff's Department had been somewhat more helpful. A bored-sounding dispatcher, who had slurped her coffee even as she spoke, had promised to pass along his message directly to the Sheriff. Regrettably, he was out in the field at that very moment. As were all of his deputies. At this time of night, Preston imagined them closing down some roadhouse or other around a pitcher of beer, but he still held out hope that the Sheriff would return his call in time to get his cars on the street.

So for now, he was on his own.

At least until the child was reported missing.

He goosed the accelerator and watched the needle top one hundred. The terrain flashed past in the darkness, rugged rock formations and vast expanses of fields interrupted by long snow-fences, only sporadically highlighted by streetlamps and limned by the occasional light of the moon when it managed to permeate the gray ceiling of clouds. He was already halfway across the state, heading northwest on Highway 287. Barring anything unforeseen, he should arrive in Lander about an hour before sunrise.

Only his intuition told him it would be too late.

V

Lander, Wyoming

Les paced the small motel room. His arm still ached from the shot of Betaseron. At least he had kept his medication in his backpack instead of his car as he'd originally intended. The last thing in the world he needed right now was for the stress to trigger an acute attack of his multiple sclerosis. Lord knew he had enough to deal with right now without winding up in the hospital.

The television droned beside him, but he had no idea what was on. He merely needed the sound of voices for company, even if he couldn't focus on the words. His students had been given a clean bill of health and a little Ativan for their anxiety, but he still bore the guilt of involving them with a heavy heart. There was no way he could have known the kind of hell they would stumble upon, but he had brought along kids who had trusted him, and whether intentionally or not, he had failed them, possibly even ruined them for their chosen field. They had initially been booked in the rooms next door to his, but Lane had managed to rouse his girlfriend from bed, and she had driven across the state to pick them up and return them to Laramie. Les was grateful they had been able to get home tonight so they could resume some semblance of normalcy in the morning.

After hours of tossing and turning because his brain refused to shut down, he had finally given up trying and decided to let his thoughts run and see where they would take him. The fact remained that the medicine wheels had originally been built for a purpose, and while the years may have scoured that purpose from the collective memory of the descendants of the ancient Native Americans who had designed them, there was obviously someone out there who at least thought he knew their function. Why else go to such great lengths to mimic a relatively obscure anthropological structure when whoever had built it could just as easily have buried the bodies in unmarked graves and been done with it? It was too convenient to think that the entire setup had been assembled simply for show. The meticulous nature of the construction and the maintenance of the site were proof enough for him, so what did its creator hope to achieve? And more importantly, why had it been necessary to involve an anthropologist, specifically him? He couldn't help but think that it was to answer the question he now pondered: What did the medicine wheel do?

Unfortunately, that answer was lost somewhere in time.

What *did* he know? The Native Americans who had first built them certainly hadn't called them by that name, an archaic term that carried negative, and arguably racist, connotations. There was a spiritual element to them, possibly in the harmony of man and nature motif. They didn't serve as protection from the elements, nor had they been designed with defensible perimeters. On the superficial level, they served as a celestial calendar, primarily to mark a single day in the year with remarkable precision on sacred land saved from snowfall only during the summer months. So what made that one day, the summer solstice, so significant? What transpired on that single day, be it spiritual or scientific, that made it so important? It was the longest day of the year, and the point at which the northern hemisphere was closest to the sun. Did that imply there were different gravitational forces at work, similar to the moon's influence on the tides? And why the corkscrew trees? What had caused them to grow in such a manner, and only in the direct vicinity of the medicine wheel? They had obviously been there before the stone creation had been erected. Were they the reason this particular location had been chosen in the first place?

His thoughts strayed to the mystical concept of energy vortices. He scoffed, but here he was contemplating gravitational pull. Could there be a relationship between the two? While the notion of a physical energy that could neither be qualified nor quantified made him roll his eyes, he couldn't argue the fact that some force other than genetics had acted upon the trees to cause the unnatural growth.

He was running in circles in his mind and accomplishing nothing. Maybe a cup of coffee would serve to sharpen his mental acuity. It couldn't hurt anyway, and the fresh air would do him some good.

There was a truck stop on the south side of the parking lot outside the motel. This whole section of town could have been dropped into the modern world from the Seventies. The motel was a blocky, two-story affair with external concrete walkways and a pool that had been filled to support a garden of dead junipers and skeletal rosebushes that stood guard over a pole that must have once flown a flag. He crossed the barren parking lot to the sprawling fuel station, a square shack from which the smell of fried eggs and burnt toast originated. A series of brightly-lit bays dominated the front of the building, housing enough pumps to fuel an entire fleet of semis, while the dirt lot behind it was packed with rows of truckers presumably sleeping in the cabs of their tractor-trailers.

A bell jangled overhead when he walked through the front door. To his left, a hairy bear of a man eyed him through the opening to the kitchen from behind a counter lined with circular stools. A plump waitress wearing a blonde wig that appeared a size too large leaned over a magazine next to the cash register. She didn't even raise her eyes. An ill-stocked convenience store consumed the other half of the building. The lights were off and no one manned the desk. He could see the empty pots on the burners at the back beside the fountain drink machines at a glance, and had to interrupt the waitress.

"Could I get a coffee to go?" he asked.

The woman's stare slowly rose from the page. She turned away from him without a word.

Les offered a smile to the short order cook, who bowed his head and returned to the griddle where he scraped at the black crust on the stainless steel.

The waitress set a paper cup in front of him and poured into it from a brown plastic carafe.

"Creamer and sugar's on the stand behind you," she said, pecking at the keys on the register.

Les watched the coffee swirl in the cup until it eventually stilled. The waitress said something, but he was still focused on his coffee. There was something about the way it had swirled...

"I said, that'll be two eighty-nine."

He slid a five across the counter. She closed it inside the drawer without offering to make change.

With a nod in her direction, he carried his cup to the condiment station, loaded it with powdered creamer and sugar, and stirred it with a tiny plastic straw. A miniature whirlpool formed, growing deeper and faster as he stirred. He paused and waited for it to settle, then twirled the straw in the opposite direction.

"Interesting."

He snatched the cup from the sticky counter and rushed out the door.

The parking lot passed in a blur as he hurried back to his room. He set the coffee on the nightstand, opened his laptop, and grabbed his digital camera from his bag. A few moments later, he had downloaded the pictures and perused them one by one. He focused on the trees. All of them spiraled counterclockwise. Every single one of them. This was no aberrant growth pattern. There had to be some kind of external force acting upon them, something centered in a radius of no more than twenty-five yards. But what kind of force could be confined to such a small, isolated region and still produce an effect strong enough to alter the genetic nature of the trees? Neither the wind nor the elements could have caused it. Radiation? The needles on the pines had appeared withered and the ground had been barren, but if that were the case, how large would the deposit of radioactive ore have to be? And surely an amount that significant would kill the trees long before triggering such a bizarre mutation, but what other forces could be locally contained?

Les thought about the coffee. With the force generated by stirring, he had created a cyclone, a spiraling vortex. He recalled the similar trees at the vortices in Sedona, Arizona. What invisible factor could make a physical object turn in a circular fashion over time? A circle inherently implied something cyclical—

His brow furrowed.

He opened the file the magnetometer had fed into his computer. The data had been reconstructed into wedge-shaped grids in hazy shades of gray; however they demonstrated streaky artifacts reminiscent of the refraction of light from the facets of an enormous gemstone. He had been distracted at the time contemplating the incongruities of the medicine wheel, but he clearly remembered Jeremy saying that he didn't think the sensing device was functioning properly. Now that he looked at the physical reconstruction of the upper strata of earth, he knew exactly what was wrong. The buried disk cases were readily apparent, as was the topsoil, which looked as though it was composed of a composite of calcite sand and ordinary dirt. But below that, the signal could reach no deeper, as though it abruptly stopped against a brick wall, which cast streaky lines throughout the entire image. It was a layer of ferromagnetic material that overloaded the signal receptors. By far the densest he had ever encountered at an archaeological site.

He leaned back and took a sip of his now cold coffee. It tasted like it had been brewed using a sweat sock for a filter.

The medicine wheel had been built on top of an incredibly large buried metal object.

But why? And more importantly, what was it?

VI

22 Miles West of Lander, Wyoming

Dandridge dialed his home number and listened to it ring while he watched the forensics techs work. They were already in the process of uncovering the fourth similarly-posed child's remains. Working counterclockwise around the outer ring of cairns, the bodies grew fresher with each subsequent disinterment. This one appeared to be the body of a young boy. His short, dark hair had receded from the exposed bone of his forehead so that his hairline was now mid-scalp, the folds of skin bunched on the back of his knobby cervical spine. Connective tissue shimmered silver on the bones like moonlight from a snake's scales. Desiccated knots of muscles and curdling clumps of adipose tissue clung in sections to the bones, which were caramel-brown with crusted blood and dirt. The broken mandible hung askew by one temporomandibular joint, the opposite temporal bone deformed by a depressed fracture that matched the one on the forehead of the girl from the video.

"Come on," he whispered as the phone continued to ring. He just needed to know that Maggie was safely asleep in her bed. Seeing these children like this, imagining what their parents must have endured, what they would feel when they learned of the ultimate fates of the children they had loved more than life itself, made him realize that mere inches of wood and sheetrock and quarter-inch panes of glass were a frighteningly inadequate defense against the horrors of the outside world. He needed to believe in the inherent decency of humanity and the fact that he stood between those rare dregs and the rest of the fundamentally good population, but this one night had shown him that true evil thrived even in his small, remote county, and he was woefully unprepared to stand against it. This killer was no man. He was a monster, the

living embodiment of everything that was wrong with mankind, a
destroyer of innocence.

He cursed when the answering machine picked up,
disconnected the call, and dialed again.

"You realize you're going to have to call in the Feds," Deputy
Miller said.

Dandridge appraised his deputy for a long moment. Miller
looked so young, so out of place. He had seen the man plunge into
the heart of brawls between men twice his size and step into the
line of fire without showing a hint of fear, but right now, he was a
terrified little boy. Dandridge wondered how *he* must look.

"Yeah. We don't have much choice in the matter, but do you
really think that will change anything?" he asked, and turned away
the moment Sharon picked up. "Why did it take so long for you to
answer?"

"It's four in the morning, Keith. Where are—?"

"Just do me a favor, okay?"

There was a pause on the other end of the line, then the click
of the bedside lamp. She must have recognized the tone of his
voice.

"What's wrong?"

"I need you to get out of bed, go down the hall, and physically
check on Maggie. I just…I just need to know she's okay."

"What's this all about? Have you been drinking?"

"I'll tell you about it when I get home. For now, it would
make me feel a lot better to know she's sleeping safely in her bed."

"Keith…"

He heard the fear in her voice, but now wasn't the time to
explain.

"Please, Sharon," he whispered. "For me."

She groaned as she rolled out of bed. He heard the squeak of
their bedroom door open, then nothing but static.

He walked past the next two cairns in the progression and
stared at the conspicuous gap in the ring. There was a pile of stones
at the edge of the forest, a haphazard jumble patiently waiting to be
assembled. The blank space frightened him more than any of the
entombed remains. It meant that somewhere out there was a child
blissfully unaware of the monster that was about to put him or her
through the worst kind of hell imaginable, through the most painful

of tortures, before he or she ended up here, bound in barbed wire and rotting—

Sharon screamed into his ear so loudly he had to pull the phone away. It felt like the ground fell out from under his feet. He staggered back toward the others, barely able to breathe, to think. Each step grew faster until he was running, the phone again pressed to his ear. His wife screamed again and started to sob.

"Maggie," she cried. "She's n-not here. And the w-window's open. Keith. The window's open!"

"Listen to me, Sharon. I need to hang up so I can call—"

"Maggie! Where is she, Keith? Where did she go?"

"Sharon." He struggled to find the air to voice his words. The path tilted from side to side as he sprinted back toward where they had parked their cars. "I have to hang up now so I can call for help. I'll be there as soon as I can."

"Sheriff," Miller called after him. "Where are you going?"

"Don't touch the window, Sharon. Don't touch anything at all. If there are fingerprints—"

"What did you do, Keith? You brought this on us, didn't you? This is your fault. Your fault!" she screamed.

Dandridge ended the call with a sob. He tripped and fell, but pushed himself back to his feet. Blood dripped from his left palm and from his knees where his slacks had torn.

The physical pain was nothing compared to what he felt inside. This had to be a nightmare. He saw an image of the terrified child bound to a particle board workbench, crying, pleading. Saw her eyes widen and heard the crack of bone when the hammer struck. Only her face was different, her hair lighter. In his mind, that child became his daughter, his Maggie, and he was helpless but to watch as she was flayed alive.

He dialed as he ran, praying to God that someone could get to his house quickly enough to catch up with whoever had stolen his daughter.

A vision of a man made of shadows stacking stones over a freshly butchered corpse, wired in repose, made him bellow in agony.

His voice echoed off into the forlorn valley and the darkness that eagerly waited to swallow it whole.

The phone continued to ring.

VII

Lander, Wyoming

Preston's Cherokee skidded to a halt in front of a light blue ranch-style house. He glanced across the street. A Saturn sedan was parked in front of a white house, just as it had been in the reflection in the photograph. He killed the engine, leapt out the door, and headed straight across the lawn toward the front door. The flowering crabapple tree stood to his right, white with blossoms; the hedgerow lined the driveway to his left. The northernmost window was wide open. He heard sirens in the distance.

The call had been relayed to his department just under twenty minutes ago and he had made the final leg of the trip at breakneck speed, navigating by his GPS unit, which had struggled to keep up with the directions. There were already two other agents en route, however neither would arrive in under three hours, and time was of the essence. The man still had a sizeable lead on him, but he would have lost time during the abduction and there was no way he would have risked driving as fast as Preston had.

He could feel it deep down in the very core of his being. Things were about to come to a head.

A blonde woman in a nightgown, her hair in rollers, threw open the front door and stumbled toward him. She was crying so hard he couldn't understand her words.

He flashed his badge and introduced himself.

"When did you first notice she was gone?" he asked, brushing past her into a comfortably furnished living room. A grandfather clock ticked in the far corner against a wall lined with family pictures, which featured the woman, Sharon Dandridge, a square-jawed man who had a former-military look, the same Sheriff he had been trying to reach for the last several hours, and the blonde girl he recognized immediately from the snapshot.

Preston turned right down the hallway toward the bedroom with the open window. The woman trailed behind him.

"I...I first noticed about...thirty minutes ago," she blubbered. "My husband...he...he...called and told me to get...get out of bed and ch-check on her. He said I needed to do it r-right that second."

Preston rounded on her and studied her face.

"Why would he wake you up and make you check on her?" he asked. "Has he ever done that before?"

The woman only shook her head.

Something must have alerted the Sheriff. Had he received Preston's message about the possible kidnapping and called home to ensure it hadn't been his child? It didn't fit. Surely Dandridge would have returned his call first.

"Where is your husband now?"

"He-he's on his way. He's been out on a case all n-night."

Preston turned to his right and stood in the doorway of the bedroom from the emailed photograph. The peach comforter and covers lay in a rumpled heap at the foot of the bed, the remaining linens fortunately unstained by blood. A bookcase to his right, posters of Hannah Montana and the Jonas Brothers. There was a desk and a dresser on the wall next to the window. The curtains fluttered inward on a faint breeze.

"Have you touched anything?" he asked.

"I...I pulled off the covers, hoping...hoping—"

"Anything else?"

"The window sill. I leaned out to see...to see if..." Her voice petered into unintelligible sobs.

Outside, the sirens grew louder and he heard the squeal of rubber on asphalt.

"Stay right there. Don't come in. Don't touch anything else."

He entered the small bedroom, which smelled of the blossoms on the tree outside the window and something else, vanilla maybe? There were no tracks on the carpet, although a full forensics analysis would find anything invisible to the naked eye, and there was no sign of a struggle. How had the man managed to take the girl from her bed and get her out the window into a waiting car

without her fighting against him or screaming loud enough to wake
the entire neighborhood? And so far, if this man was a serial child
abductor as Preston suspected, he had never been so bold as to
break into the house. All of his previous victims had been taken
outside of their homes. This was an escalation in his M.O.. Why
would he change it so suddenly, especially after tipping his hand to
Preston with the email? Did that imply an element of diminishing
time?

Alternating shades of red and blue strobed the room through
the window. Tires screeched and the sirens died. He heard the
crackle of radios, then the clap of footsteps on the sidewalk.

He glanced back at the doorway, which was now empty. The
woman must have headed for the front door to let the officers in.
Good. Let them take her statement while he scoured the room. The
man who had sent the email had wanted him here first for a reason.
There had to be a clue as to why. It couldn't be as simple as the
man thumbing his nose at him for being unable to catch him. There
was a purpose for drawing him into the chase when he had been no
closer to even sniffing the perpetrator's trail than ever before. It
was as though he wanted Preston to catch him, but why now? Why
after all this time?

Voices reverberated through the walls from the living room.

Preston inched closer to the window. The hamper to his left
was overflowing, the arm of a sweatshirt spilling over the rim. A
giant stuffed bear sat in the corner, a Brats doll on each leg. He
leaned over the sill, careful not to so much as brush against it, and
scrutinized it for visible prints in the accumulation of dust, but it
was relatively clean and free of any significant marks. Possibly a
proper dusting and black light canvassing would turn up prints or
fluids of some kind.

He looked down at the ground outside the window. Small
white petals were evenly scattered across the lawn, save for one
spot directly in front of him, where they appeared to have been
mounded.

Preston chewed on his lower lip while he thought.

The voices approached from behind and he heard footsteps in
the hallway.

Preston turned and left the room. He passed Mrs. Dandridge
and a uniformed officer who barely appeared out of his teens on

his way to the living room, where two more uniforms had begun to unload tackle boxes filled with evidence collecting gear. Another officer was cordoning off the front yard with crime scene tape when he emerged from the front door and carefully eased along the face of the house toward the open window. The grass was matted in spots, but there were no obvious footprints. When he was within reach of the small pile of petals, he extricated his pen from his pocket and gently brushed away the uppermost petals until he uncovered a bundled swatch of fabric. He peeked from the corner of his eye at the officer, who now had his back to him as he rounded the mailbox on the street, then carefully teased the cloth out of the pile. It was worn and dirty, but the fabric was unmistakable. A black satin that iridesced with indigo when he tilted it toward the streetlight.

Tears brimmed in his eyes and his vision momentarily blurred.

It was a tattered swatch of the dress Savannah had been wearing the last time he had seen her.

And beneath it was a small plastic 16 gigabyte USB flash drive.

He set down the frayed swatch and noticed that several words had been written on it in silver fabric marker, all block letters. Something inside of him broke and a sorrow beyond anything he had ever experienced tightened around his heart.

Preston could only stare at the words.

SHE CRIED FOR HER DADDY.

VIII

Les studied the magnetometer readings. The metallic object consumed the lower strata of each of the sections they'd surveyed. He could only assume that whatever was buried down there was as large as the entire clearing, and it only stood to reason that it could have contributed to the aberrant tree growth. But what could it be? Unfortunately, the layer of metal distorted the signal of anything that might be hidden beneath it. For all he knew, it could merely be a quarter-inch thick, or it could be a solid block that extended halfway to the earth's core. What he could tell, however, was that the surface they had imaged was reasonably flat and horizontal, which excluded even the densest lode of naturally occurring ferromagnetic material. Without a doubt, the object was manmade. It obviously predated the medicine wheel built on top of it, but it had to have been buried there long after the Native Americans who had initially constructed the wagon wheel designs had stopped making them.

He thought about the surface soil. There was no discoloration to suggest it had been turned anytime recently, other than over the small sections where the DVDs had been buried. The dirt had been solidly packed, and while he was no expert on determining the age of trees, they had definitely been growing there for quite some time. He did know that pines were notoriously slow growers, but with the way the trunks corkscrewed, it was impossible to tell how they compared in height to those in the surrounding forest if they were uncoiled. And since their growth patterns were affected by an external force, then surely the rate must have been as well. The trees weren't nearly as dense in that circular clearing, which suggested they may have once been razed to allow for the metallic object's construction.

And just like that, he was right back where he started. He couldn't figure out what could be causing the potential electromagnetic disturbance any more than he could divine the identity of the buried object.

Perhaps he was approaching this quandary from the wrong angle. Neither physics nor forestry could be counted among his strengths. Maybe since whoever had built the medicine wheel had a solid background in anthropology, the answers he sought could be found somewhere in his field of expertise. After all, whoever had sent him the photographs had gone to considerable lengths to ensure the presence of an anthropologist.

He initiated one internet search after another. The various myths surrounding the origin of the medicine wheel speculated that they were designed by the Plains Indians to commune with their Creator, perform various healing ceremonies, and conduct rituals of all kinds. He couldn't imagine how they could be used for these purposes now, so he investigated solar calendars in general, everything from Stonehenge to the Carocal Observatory in the Mayan ruins at Chichén Itzá. Their purpose was to mark celestial events, but didn't appear to have a functional component beyond that. There were twenty-eight cairns, which corresponded with the cycle of the moon. Unfortunately, he could find little correlation outside of superstition for the number as it pertained to medicine wheels. He had already searched the growth patterns of the trees, so what did that leave?

His coffee cup was now empty, but the last thing he wanted was to return to that dive. He'd felt about as welcome as the stomach flu, and he didn't like the odds that they had brewed a fresh pot since he left. Soon enough, the sun would rise, and from there it was only a matter of time before he would be free to pick up his car and head back to Laramie. Maybe he should just call it a night, grab what little sleep he could, and try to forget about this whole mess. However, he knew that turning his back on a mystery once his curiosity was aroused simply wasn't in his nature.

He was just about to take a walk in hopes that the cool night air would clear his head and provide some inspiration when he realized there was one angle he hadn't carefully considered. The bodies. Until that moment, he had thought of them as separate from the medicine wheel itself, a macabre symptom of a diseased mind. Was it possible that whoever buried them in the cairns perceived them as instrumental to its function?

Quick searches of a dozen variations of "corpses" and "medicine wheels" led him to nothing of significance. He added the criteria of "summer solstice" and "children." This time, there were some interesting matches.

He clicked the first link, and opened a page from the site of the University of Alberta's Cultural Anthropology Department. At the top, there was a picture of an ancient carving in limestone. It reminded him of many of the primitive Native American petroglyphs: two-dimensional, almost abstract renderings of stick figures. The petroglyph had been discovered on a sheer cliff near Lake Louise in Banff National Park only two years ago, and had yet to be attributed to a specific tribe, especially considering how many had lived in the dense pine forests and steep mountainous valleys over the course of the last ten thousand years. The author of the short article beneath the image suspected it had been carved by either the Blackfoot or the Shoshone, who were credited for many of the petroglyphs across the province.

The etching depicted the sun at the top, roughly twenty-five degrees to the right of the center of the design. The earth was represented by a straight line with a gap in the middle. There were small stick figures to either side of the break in the horizontal line, beneath which was a square pit. A larger stick figure stood at the bottom, and above his head, wavy lines connected him to a larger stick figure still, which hovered between the level of the ground and the sun. Dozens of spirals had been carved under the diminutive stick figures, all of them counterclockwise, a traditional motif among indigenous tribes, who often carved them along particularly treacherous trails or at the entrance to perilous canyons. It was the sign for danger. And coincidentally, it just happened to match the spiral orientation of the strange trees. There were several more smaller spirals in the sky amid a scattering of stars. The entire design was enclosed inside a circle with dots along its circumference like the outer ring of a medicine wheel.

Les skimmed the article. It was all speculation without any substantiated fact. The author, a graduate student named Patricia Christensen, suspected the petroglyph represented a ritual that corresponded to the summer solstice, as evidenced by the angle of the sun to the horizon, twenty-six degrees to match that of the celestial orb, which reached its northernmost position relative to the earth over the Tropic of Cancer on that day. The stars were supposedly Aldebaran, Fomalhaut, Rigel, and Sirius, among others. But there was no mention of the possible significance of the smaller stick figures, whose size suggested they might be children, nor of the odd relationship between the man in the pit and the other in the sky.

He clicked through a few more sites, which were all variations upon the same theme. While the order of the words changed, their substance and the picture never did.

Les rubbed his weary eyes and glanced toward the curtains. The night had brightened considerably, but the sun had yet to breach the eastern horizon on this summer solstice. Who knew what this, the longest day of the year, would bring? All he knew with any kind of certainty was that whoever had built the medicine wheel and summoned him all the way out here into the Wind River Range had meant to mark this one day, but for what reason?

He again looked at his laptop and gasped.

The layer of ferromagnetic material under the ground.

The larger stick figure in the pit on the petroglyph.

Fumbling the business card the deputy had given him from his wallet, he reached for the phone.

Jesus.

He suddenly realized why he'd been drawn into this mess.

He knew how to find the killer.

Chapter Three

I

22 Miles West of Lander, Wyoming

Deputy Sean Miller walked to the western edge of the clearing. He heard what sounded like a distant scream echo off into the darkened valley. His mind was playing tricks on him now. The more he rehearsed the sound in his head, the more certain he became that it had just been the cry of a circling hawk. This crime scene was really starting to get to him. All of the death and the hideous manner in which the bodies had been staged was like something out of his worst nightmares. This definitely wasn't what he'd signed on for. He needed to get away from the carnage, if only for a few minutes. Just take a quick break to get some fresh air and calm his nerves. He was already starting to feel as though the children they disinterred one by one were somehow watching him from the corners of their vacant eyes.

He glanced over his shoulder to confirm that the others were still occupied by their various tasks, then ducked off into the forest. Once he was far enough away that he could no longer smell the worsening stench of decomposition, he stood on top of a rocky ledge and stared down into the canyon. The sky had begun to lighten by degree overhead. A thin stream meandered through the dense pines far below. Rugged granite outcroppings formed steep walls on the opposite side, beyond which sharp mountain peaks serrated the western horizon. He plucked a Doral from his pack and lit it, allowing the smoke to momentarily cleanse him and take the edge off his nerves.

The Sheriff had run off without explanation nearly two hours ago now and still hadn't passed along word of his whereabouts to them. For all they knew, Dandridge had cracked up and abandoned them. He knew Keith better than that, though. They'd worked together for nearly three years now. His sudden disappearance was totally out of character. Something must have happened elsewhere in the county that required the Sheriff's immediate attention, although Miller couldn't imagine anything more pressing than their current situation. Had Keith mentioned something about waking up his wife to check on their daughter? Was something wrong with Maggie? For now he could only guess. The Sheriff had taken the satellite phone, effectively cutting them off from the outside world. They were well outside of cell phone range and this high in the mountains their walkie-talkies were useless. Maybe he could use that as an excuse to hoof it back down to his cruiser to check in with dispatch.

He drew the last drag from his cigarette, crushed the cherry under his heel, and launched the butt out over the nothingness.

The prospect of returning to the ring of corpses made him physically ill, but the sooner this was all over, the better. He was going to do whatever it took to get back to his normal life and a nice hot shower if he had to bag every last one of those festering skeletons and carry them down the mountain himself. Whatever it took to get him out of this damn forest, which had begun to feel as though it was sucking the very life out of him.

Miller started back toward the clearing. It announced its proximity to his olfactory senses first. Dear God, was it possible that the smell had grown even worse in the few minutes he'd been gone? He heard the clatter of stones being cast aside from the cairns and muffled voices from directly ahead, and unconsciously slowed his pace. Surely at some point in the coming morning another deputy would be dispatched to spell him, if only long enough to get a few hours of sleep. It was a good thing news of their discovery hadn't leaked. Lord only knew what kind of hell might break loose if the mice learned that all of the cats were away.

He was nearly to the clearing when he caught a glimpse of blue from the corner of his eye. Around the thick trunk of a ponderosa pine, he could barely see the shoulder and hip of one of the uniformed officers. Hank Wilcox was squatting with his back against the tree.

Miller chuckled.

"Hey, Wilcox. What are you doing back there? Taking a dump?"

He waited for a response that never came. Not even a grunt. And Wilcox made no effort to maneuver himself out of sight.

"Come on. You know I'm just giving you shit. Or do you have plenty of that back there already?"

Miller shoved through a stand of scrub oak and rounded the trunk. Wilcox leaned against the bark, legs tucked against his chest, forehead resting on his knees. Was that shifty little bastard trying to sneak a catnap?

"Give me a break, man. If I have to stay awake and rummage through corpses, then so do..." His voice petered to a whisper. "Holy crap."

Wilcox's slacks were splotched with black stains and his face was smeared with what Miller at first assumed was mud. He tipped up Wilcox's chin. Vacuous brown eyes stared through him. A gaping laceration crossed the officer's throat, from which a steady trickle of blood flowed.

"Jesus," Miller gasped, dropping Wilcox's head back against his knees.

Miller's heart raced. He drew his pistol with trembling hands and sighted the forest down the barrel. The killer was out there somewhere at this very moment. His first instinct was to shout for help, but the last thing he wanted was to draw attention to himself and betray his location. The killer already had every other advantage.

He walked slowly back to the path, careful not to make even a single twig snap underfoot. A gentle breeze shivered through the canopy and rustled the detritus. Several more stones clattered before the sounds ceased altogether.

Silence washed over the forest.

Miller crept forward, arms extended, sweeping his pistol from side to side. A gateway of twisted pines welcomed him into the clearing. Everything was still. The rotten remains of children knelt at the perimeter, some amid the piles of rocks hauled away from the cairns, others still entombed. His skin crawled beneath the weight of unseen eyes. He couldn't shake the feeling that the small skulls turned imperceptibly to watch him pass.

He surveyed the area. The cases of evidence-collecting gear lay on the ground, their contents spilled across the dirt beside a broken laptop. One of the cairns to the north was arrested in a state of partial deconstruction. Only the cranium and a portion of the right shoulder were visible through the gap. A cloud of dust settled over a patch of disturbed pine needles. All of the others were gone, simply vanished.

Again, he resisted the urge to call out and eased silently toward the jumble of gear. It wasn't until he was nearly right on top of it that he saw the amoeboid patches of mud surrounding the cairn. Arcs of dark fluid crisscrossed the mound of stones and drew lines across the earth.

Panic seized him. The others had been slaughtered right here, and they hadn't seen it coming. He hadn't heard a single gunshot, which would have reverberated through the mountains like a peal of thunder. There were no signs of a struggle, other than the scuff marks in the dirt and—

Smooth trails led into the forest behind the cairn, thick with mud and lined with the disturbed detritus. Something had been dragged off into the underbrush. Something that was still bleeding.

He pointed his Beretta Px4 Storm at the wall of pines, aspens, and the scrub oak between their coiled trunks, and advanced slowly. His pulse thumped in his ears so hard and fast it caused his vision to tremble, lending movement to the leaves and branches, and the shadows lurking beneath them. Every instinct cried out for him to turn around and run as fast as he could in the opposite direction, but none of these men, these trained law enforcement officers, had been given enough warning of the impending attack to fire off a round in their defense, let alone raise a cry for help. If he ran, he would be sacrificing the small measure of power he maintained with the pistol.

At the edge of the forest, he shouldered aside the branches that obstructed the course of the bloody trail and gasped in shock. A haphazard mound of bodies had been heaped on a mat of dead leaves, a tangle of arms and legs that smelled of freshly butchered meat. Vacant eyes. Startled expressions. Torn clothing. And more blood than he had ever seen before.

Miller staggered backward toward the cairn, turning in circles with his weapon raised. Forget trying to gain control of the situation. Six men had been slain in the time it had taken him to smoke a cigarette. This was now about survival.

He heard a muffled scream. It sounded as though it had come from miles away, only there had been no echo. And it hadn't originated in the wilderness, but from somewhere much, much closer.

Stepping over the short rock spokes of the wagon wheel design, he took the most direct route to the path that would eventually guide him back to where he had left his car.

Another scream. Tortured, horrible, pitiful. And the voice had sounded so young...

This time there was no denying where it had come from.

He glanced toward the mouth of the distant path and debated making a break for it until another dampened scream made the decision for him. Breathing fast, on the verge of hyperventilating, he turned in the direction from which the cries had come, and slowly advanced toward the central cairn. Another scream, still muffled, but he was certain it had risen from inside that central ring of stones.

Dawn announced its impending arrival from behind the mutated trees against the eastern horizon, a blood-red stain to match the horrors of the night.

Miller crept up onto a twisted trunk and leaned over the rim of the piled stones.

A scream came from directly below him, attenuated by the earth.

He looked down and saw only a layer of dirt scuffed by indistinct footprints. Wait. The ground appeared cracked. No, not cracked. Carved. There was a perfect, circular—

Dark fluid spattered down on the dirt a heartbeat before he felt the pressure against his neck, pressure that quickly transformed into pain. His Beretta fell from his grasp and landed in the bottom of the cairn with a clang. A metallic taste filled his mouth. His breathing became labored. He heard a gurgling sound and clasped his hands over his slick throat. His fingers slipped deep inside the wound, grazing exposed muscles, tendons, and the coarse ring of his rapidly filling trachea.

Blackness converged from the corners of his vision. He spun around and fell from his perch. The ground rose to meet him, pounding his face with a solid *crunch* that marred his dwindling field of view with starbursts.

Hands closed around his ankles and hauled him in reverse. His life fled him with the blood that warmed his face and trailed away from him in a muddy smear.

II

Lander, Wyoming

Preston sat in the passenger seat of his Jeep with his computer open on his lap. He turned the USB flash drive over and over in his hand. For the hundredth time, he glanced out the window to make sure that he hadn't aroused suspicion. Eventually, he would turn in the memory stick and fabric sample as evidence, but for now, it was a message left specifically for him, and he needed to be the one to decipher it. If he could summon the strength to open whatever files were contained on the device.

The officer who had been stringing the crime scene tape had finished his task and now worked the perimeter, chasing off concerned neighbors and one curious early morning jogger, who ran in place while he tried to talk the details out of the uniform. The others were still inside, presumably taking the mother's statement, dusting for prints, and collecting evidence, minus the only shred Preston knew they would find, which he now plugged into the port on his laptop. He held his breath while he waited for the list of files to pop up. When the system finally recognized the input, it showed only a single file had been saved onto the portable storage device.

The name of the file was 4.6-20.SS.

He gently stroked the silky fabric, drawing a measure of comfort from it despite its message, as he double-clicked the file and waited for it to open.

The acids in his stomach seethed and he felt a sharp cramp in his gut.

His media player opened and expanded to fill the screen. A large black view window above a row of playback controls stared blankly back at him.

What was he preparing to watch? Was it a recorded message from the man who had stolen his child? Would he finally get to see the monster's face? Was it possible that despite the words written on the swatch torn from her dress that Savannah was still alive and her abductor wanted to flaunt his superiority or just further string him along?

He needed to find out. Every waking minute of the last six years had been devoted to learning what had happened to his daughter and finding the man who had taken her from him. And now, here he sat, in what felt like a different life entirely from the one he had shared with his wife and child, prepared to do just that.

His hand shook so badly he could barely align the cursor with the PLAY button. With one final peek out the window to make sure no one was watching, he tapped the mouse button and the film started to roll.

He held out what little hope remained inside of him like a helpless, blind, newborn mouse, and forced himself to breathe. Soon enough, the officers inside would wonder why he was sitting out in his car when he should be in there with them, taking the lead. He needed to hurry, but he couldn't allow himself to miss a single word, a single detail—

There was a crackle of static. Or had it been commotion off-screen? He heard a whimper and recognized Savannah's tiny voice immediately. Even had he not watched their old home movies over and over, her voice was ingrained into his very soul. He felt the terror in that single whimper, an icicle driven through his heart. There was a loud clatter, and then his baby started to scream.

"Oh God," he whispered. "Please don't. Please…"

A single light bulb bloomed with a snap and the camera drifted out of focus before rectifying again. The bronze glare illuminated a small room with bare cinder block walls decorated with black arcs and spatters. Cobwebs swayed from the ceiling. A dark silhouette with a long head and stooped shoulders was framed in the center. It leaned away from the camera and his daughter screamed. In one swift motion, the man ducked out of sight, leaving Preston with the fleeting glimpse of sagging ears and a bulbous nose in profile. A green chalkboard blotted out the view. The same combination of numbers and letters from the file name were written on it. And then it was gone.

Preston sobbed out loud.

There. On a workbench built from particle board. Savannah. Bound to the table by her wrists and ankles with thick, frayed rope. Naked. Bruised. Her skin covered with filth. Trembling. Whimpering.

Preston looked directly into her wide eyes, saw the fear, the horror, the pain, and something inside of him broke. Tears streamed from his eyes. He felt as though he were being torn apart from the inside out. The last of his hope was yanked from his grasp by cruel talons that ripped it to bloody shreds before his very eyes.

"Daddy," his daughter cried. "Where's my daddy? I want to go home. Please. I need to see my mommy. Take me...take me home. Please."

He wanted to crawl out of his skin. No child should have to endure something like...this. And no parent should be forced to watch.

With a metallic clamor, a cart covered with a display of rusted surgical implements rolled in from the left side of the screen. The shadowed man stepped in front of his baby girl and perused the utensils one at a time, tracing a finger along the contours of each, almost lovingly. When he finally settled upon the one he wanted, he lifted it from the towel-draped tray and turned toward Savannah. The tip of the scalpel glinted and screams erupted from the speakers.

Preston had to turn away. He couldn't bear to watch, even though he knew he should. This had all been his fault, and he should have been able to take the pain in her stead. But he couldn't...couldn't watch the child he loved more than anything he had ever known be made to suffer in a way that no loving God would ever allow.

He rubbed the smooth fabric between his fingers and stared through tear-blurred eyes at the sun rising over the houses across the street while he listened to his daughter call out for him from across time and from beyond the grave, listened to her beg for him to come and save her, to take her home, to make the pain stop. He listened to her scream in agony, beyond the point where she could even form words.

There was a loud *crack* that he felt as much as heard.

And then his daughter, his beautiful Savannah, cried no more.

Over his own sobs, Preston heard sounds like duct tape being ripped away from skin and the panting breathing of the man laboring, hard at work.

He bared his teeth and slammed his elbow into the side window. A spider web of cracks splintered away from the point of impact. He bellowed a mixture of emotions he could no longer control.

His hands curled to fists and his teeth ground with a screech. He was going to hunt down the man who had done this to his daughter, and he was going to destroy him, body and soul.

Nothing else mattered.

It was all he had left to live for now.

III

Les had already tried calling every number he could think of several times. The number on the card Deputy Henson had given him had only reached voicemail, and both the police and sheriff's department dispatchers had promised to have someone call him back as soon as they could. Unfortunately, neither sounded as though they believed a word he said. Apparently, the majority of the available manpower was already at the site and outside of radio range. In such a small county and even smaller town, they were understaffed and unprepared for the kind of emergency they now faced. Les didn't know what to do. If he was right, then the killer was already in their midst and he could only speculate as to the significance of the solstice to the man who had staged the frightening burials.

He felt caged. He needed to get out of there, get the blood circulating through his brain again, but at the same time, he didn't want to stray too far from the phone in case someone finally returned his call. His car was impounded and he couldn't imagine there were any car rental agencies anywhere nearby, at least none that would be open this early in the morning. What was he going to do anyway, drive back up the mountain to pass along his suspicions? The prospect of returning to the medicine wheel, especially if the killer was already waiting there for them scared the hell out of him. But he couldn't stand idly by while something terrible happened either.

Why did he feel any sort of responsibility anyway? This wasn't his problem. He had simply been the unlucky one who had stumbled upon that horrible clearing. Yet someone had wanted him to. Why? It didn't make the slightest bit of sense for a criminal to call attention to his crimes. Did he want to get caught? No way. That didn't stand to reason. The man had wanted his work to be discovered by someone who would potentially understand its significance. Was he merely trying to show off, or did Les have a part to play in the endgame?

He should just find the nearest Greyhound station and hop a bus back home. After all, he'd done nothing wrong, and if the police needed him to answer more questions, they knew where to find him. It wasn't as though he was going to make a break for the border.

But he knew what it boiled down to. Professional curiosity. It was an anthropologist's Achilles' heel. He had entered this profession because there were so many questions for which there were no easy answers. There were so many societies that had made their mark on the planet and then just disappeared. What could have caused a primitive culture capable of charting the patterns and orbits of celestial bodies millions of miles away to vanish into thin air? And currently of greater importance, what was the function of the medicine wheel, an elaborate construct built to foretell a single date in a time before calendars, and why had one been erected now, hundreds of years after its meaning had been lost to the ages?

He again turned his attention to the picture of the petroglyph. Many Native American cultures believed that they were birthed from the heart of the earth and rose to the surface, where their Creator awaited them in a world of his conception. It almost appeared as though the larger of the stick figures was in the process of ascending, being born not onto the same plane as the assembly of smaller figures gathered to bear witness, but into a higher level of existence altogether, possibly a godlike state. Surely the wavy lines implied some sort of movement or maybe even metamorphosis, but when taken in a modern context, its implied meaning fell apart. Someone out there, however, obviously believed in its theoretical function. Was this person following the design like a blueprint in an attempt to undergo some sort of spiritual or physical ascension? Les shook his head. A man would have to be out of his mind to think in such a way, but any man who was capable of killing twenty-eight children in order to recreate a rite depicted in a petroglyph etched more than a thousand years ago had left his right mind long ago.

Les paused. There had been a conspicuous gap in the outer ring of the medicine wheel. Twenty-seven cairns, not twenty-eight.

For the man who had set up this whole scenario to finish the wheel, he still needed one more body. Was it possible that at this very moment a child was in mortal danger? Was there a terrified little boy or girl down there in the pit with him right now? Was that child already dead?

He couldn't wait around any longer. Time was flowing past and he would never be able to forgive himself if his inaction proved to be the death of an innocent child.

Grabbing his laptop and tucking it under his arm, he raced toward the door. He patted his pocket to make sure he had his cell phone and closed the door behind him. The rising sun barely peered over the eastern horizon, a red stain that faded to blue overhead and then finally to black to the west, where the stars dissolved into nothingness. Across the parking lot, several interstate truckers fueled their tanks. More milled around the rigs parked in the rear, preparing once again to hit the road after an uncomfortable night's rest.

Les ran to the closest trucker, a scrawny man who wore a flannel shirt, dirty Levis, and a hat that sat way too high on his head. The man had just hung the nozzle back on the pump and was about to haul himself up into the red Kenmore cab.

"Hey," Les called. "I need a lift just up to the end of Country Road Nineteen. Can you help me—?"

"I'm headed south from here and have to be in Denver by three if I hope to have any help on the loading dock. Sorry, man. I wish I could help you out, but time's money."

"I'll pay you fifty bucks."

The trucker shook his head, smiled not unsympathetically, and climbed up into his cab without another word.

"Damn it," Les snapped. "A child is in serious danger. I need—"

The slamming door cut him off.

He was just about to run toward the trucker in the next bay when a voice called out from his right.

"Fifty bucks to get you up to CR Nineteen, you say?"

Les spun to see the short order cook who had eyed him from the kitchen in the diner hours ago.

"Yeah. Will you do it?"

"Let me see the cash."

Les fished out his wallet and removed all of the bills. He sifted through the small stack of tens, fives, and ones.

"I only have forty-eight."

"That'll do," the man said, plucking the money from Les's hand and leading him back around the side of the building to where an old Ford F-150 pickup waited. The white paint had turned the color of dirt, the wheel wells were rusted into intricate lattices, and the tires were so bald that the belts showed through the rubber.

Les hurried around to the passenger side and climbed in the moment the cook unlocked the door.

"Thanks," he said. "I can't tell you how much I appreciate this."

The cook nodded and gunned the engine, which knocked so badly it felt as though the entire vehicle were being peppered with bullets. Thirty seconds later, they were skidding sideways out of the dirt lot and onto the asphalt.

Les pried his cell phone from the pocket of his pants and tried dialing the same numbers again. Maybe he'd get lucky and actually get to talk to a real live officer. If not, then soon enough he would make them listen, face-to-face.

IV

Dandridge slammed the brakes and skidded into his driveway, tearing through the police tape and nearly running down the officer in the process. He leapt out the door of the Blazer and sprinted toward the front door. Sharon ran from the living room and met him on the front porch, where she collapsed into his arms. She sobbed uncontrollably, but he couldn't find the words to console her. Not now. The run down the mountainside had helped him focus his panic and helplessness into determination. There was no time to allow his emotions to get in the way. Someone had taken his daughter from inside his house, and if he ever wanted to see her again, he was going to have to find her in a hurry. He knew that the element of time was crucial in cases like this. Even traveling at the speed limit, such a large head start could place his little girl nearly a hundred miles away in any direction; however, for whatever reason, he thought not. He would have checkpoints set up on all of the major highways regardless, but he was certain that whoever abducted Maggie—a sheriff's daughter for Christ's sake—was the same man who had erected the tableau of death. Call it deductive reasoning or just gut instinct. The man intended to keep Maggie close, and he was going to do unthinkable things to her if Dandridge didn't find her right now.

He shed his wife and hurried into the house. Sharon wailed and grabbed for him, but he jerked his arm away. She fell to the ground and cried out for him. The pain in her voice tore him up inside.

"Have you found anything?" he asked as he entered the living room. His walkie-talkie squawked for what seemed like the thousandth time and he silenced it. He spent every day of his life helping every damn person in the county with their inane problems. Right now, he had his own and everything else was just going to have to wait. Drunks could drive off into ditches and couples could scream and beat the heck out of each other for all he cared. He was going to find Maggie if it cost him his job, and he was going to kill the son of a bitch for having the audacity to even touch his child.

"We found a good number of viable prints in the bedroom, but we'll have to wait for the lab to prepare an analysis," the officer said. He sat on the couch like he owned the place, still holding his notebook in his hands. Dandridge's arrival must have interrupted his wife's statement. "We have to make sure they don't belong to either you or your wife first."

"Any other...samples?" Dandridge cringed when he said it. They all knew what he meant by samples. Blood, tissue, fibers...semen.

"No, sir."

Without another word, Dandridge rushed down the hall and into Maggie's bedroom. An officer knelt below the window, combing through the carpet with tweezers under the purple glow of a black light. He took in the room at a glance: rumpled bed linens on the floor; nothing broken; window open and intact; no blood or outward signs of a struggle.

As he neared, he noticed the car parked on the curb outside the tape in front of his house. There was a silhouette inside, framed against the glare of the rising sun. He had been in such a hurry to get into the house that he hadn't even noticed the Cherokee canted up on the sidewalk.

"Who's in the Jeep outside?"

"Federal Agent," the officer said without raising his eyes. "He was already here when we arrived."

"Why's he just sitting out there in his car?"

"Beats the hell out of me. He's been like that for a while now. We figured we'd just leave him to it. Buy ourselves some time to do our jobs before this turns into a sideshow, you know?"

Dandridge knew exactly what the officer meant. There was no time for a messy debate over jurisdiction or to bring anyone new up to speed. But what troubled him most was that a Federal Agent had been the first on the scene at a house not far from the middle of nowhere within a matter of minutes after Sharon called nine-one-one. The man would have to have been within miles of his house to beat the police here, and he couldn't think of a single good reason for that. What did the agent know, and why in the name of God was he just sitting out there in his damn car when Maggie could be anywhere by now?

"You let me know the second you find anything," Dandridge said. He stormed out of the room and nearly barreled through his wife on the way out of the house. Focusing on the unmoving shape in the Cherokee, he strode right up to the driver's side door and looked through the window.

A man in his late thirties, wearing a disheveled suit, sat in the passenger seat with an open laptop on his thighs. He stared blankly through the front windshield, tears glistening on his cheeks. Dandridge could hear him crying even through the closed door. He craned his neck so he could see the monitor and did a double-take.

He threw open the door and leaned across the driver's seat.

"Where did you get that?" There was no way any of that footage could have leaked from his crime scene so quickly. This agent had arrived at his house far too quickly, and now here he was watching a video there was no way he should have had.

The man turned toward him with a startled expression.

Dandridge grabbed him by the jacket, yanked him across the seat, and bared his teeth. "Where did you get that?"

"On the ground outside the window," the man whispered, holding out a weathered tatter of fabric. "It was wrapped in this." Dandridge released the agent's jacket, snatched the swatch from him, and read the inscription. "It's a scrap of fabric from the dress my daughter was wearing when she was abducted six years ago."

"And you found this here?" Dandridge asked in a softer tone. He held the cloth out for the man, who nodded and tucked it carefully into his jacket pocket. "Along with that video." Again the man nodded. Dandridge looked into the agent's teary eyes and asked the question he had no choice but to ask. "And the child on the recording?"

"Her name was Savannah. She would have been sixteen years old yesterday." There was a rustling sound from the laptop. A bright glow bloomed from the little girl's chest, almost like the reflection of the sun from glass, and then the footage went black. A puzzled expression crossed the man's face. "You've seen a recording like this one before?"

Dandridge studied the man, but betrayed nothing.

"I want to know how it is that a Federal Agent with Colorado license plates was the first person to arrive at my house. You'd better tell me everything you know, and don't even try to bullshit me. My daughter is missing, and if anything happens to her, I'll skin you alive. You understand?"

"Tell me where you saw a video like this and I'll give you everything I have."

"I don't have time for this! My daughter is out there somewhere with—"

"The same man who killed *my* daughter!"

Dandridge drew his Beretta and pointed it between the agent's eyes.

"If you know where he took her, you'd better tell me this very second or so help me I'll put a bullet through your head right now!"

"Tell me where you saw the video!"

The look in the man's eyes told Dandridge he had witnessed enough suffering that he didn't fear the pistol. He had no other choice.

"There were more of them. Buried in the mountains. By the bodies."

The agent closed his eyes for a long moment before opening them again. The tears stopped and his face hardened.

"Take me there, and I'll help you find your daughter."

"Sheriff Dandridge?" an officer interrupted from just outside the open driver's side door.

"What?" he snapped, pulling the gun away from the agent's forehead.

"A man named Lester Grant has been trying to get a hold of you. I just got word from dispatch. He says he knows where to find the killer."

"Get in," the agent said, nearly shoving Dandridge out of the car as he hopped across the console into the driver's seat. His laptop clattered to the floor as he cranked the key and revved the engine.

Dandridge sprinted around the hood and jumped in through the passenger side door, already dialing the motel's number on his cell phone.

The Cherokee peeled away from the curb and rocketed to the north.

"Now," Dandridge said as the dial tone droned in his ear. "Talk."

V

22 Miles West of Lander, Wyoming

All of the cars, minus the Sheriff's Blazer, were still parked exactly where they had been when Henson drove him to the motel, only all of the sirens were now dark. Les had hoped to find at least one of the officers milling around the lot so he could simply relay his message and be done with it, but his luck held true. He dreaded the prospect of hiking back up to that site. The last thing he wanted was to see how many more corpses they'd uncovered during the night. Or worse still, if he was right and the killer was up there at this very moment, he feared the thought of running into him in the middle of the isolated wilderness. Surely there were enough policemen up there that even if the killer was hiding where Les suspected, he wouldn't dare take the chance of revealing his presence. Les just needed to reach the officers, tell them what his research produced, and then allow himself to be escorted back to town, where surely his car would be waiting for him and he could return to his normal life. Before the start of the evening news, he'd be lounging in his recliner with a well-deserved glass of wine, this whole mess already forgotten.

Of course, that didn't make his current task any less terrifying.

The grumble of the old pickup faded behind him, leaving him to the company of the raucous starlings and the squeaking ground squirrels. He stared up the steep first leg of the path to where it disappeared into the pines. The sooner he started, the sooner he'd be back down here, he told himself. And while the shadows still clung to the forest, at least he wasn't making this journey under the dead of night in complete darkness.

He drew a measure of comfort from the sunlight. Monsters only hunted at night, didn't they? But that was another thing that troubled him. He may have discovered the ancient schematics for the medicine wheel, but he still had no idea what its function might be. What was the construct's relationship to today, the summer solstice, and how did it relate to the proximity of the sun? And there were still the trees to consider. What was buried under the ground that had caused such strange growth patterns?

A shiver rippled up his spine. The branches above him swayed against the cool morning breeze.

He was just going to have to wait and watch the news for resolution. Right now, his only concern was making sure the police were properly prepared to roust the killer from his warren so there wouldn't be another body to complete the outer ring of the medicine wheel, and then he could formally wash his hands of it.

As the golden sun rose slowly in the sky, Les mounted the trail, doing his best to focus on anything other than the image of twenty-eight small bodies bearing witness to the ascension of something dark from the pit.

VI

13 Miles West of Lander, Wyoming

Preston pinned the gas pedal coming out of the curve and into a short, rutted straightaway. Gravel ricocheted from the undercarriage. The tires slewed from side to side, throwing up a roiling cloud of dust in their wake. The professor's motel room had been empty when they arrived, however his belongings were still heaped in the corner. He hadn't mentioned where he might have gone to the desk clerk who had opened the room for them, and they hadn't had the time to canvass the town looking for him. With the Sheriff's daughter already in the clutches of the killer, their only option was to follow their instincts, and they both agreed that going to the site of the awful burial was the most logical course of action considering they had no other leads.

Preston tried to steel himself against the horrible reality of coming face-to-face with his daughter's posed remains, but he knew there was nothing he could do to mentally prepare himself. He had already witnessed the worst of it, but the camera lens tended to create a barrier of unreality between the atrocity and the viewer. The grim truth would set in when he finally saw what was left of Savannah with his own eyes, when he finally touched the decomposed skin of the cheek he had kissed so many times.

An old Ford pickup barreled around the bend and nearly sideswiped them. Preston managed to hug the slanted shoulder and the edge of the forest at the last second.

"Jesus," Dandridge said from the seat beside him. The Sheriff braced one hand on the dashboard and clung to the door handle with the other. All of the color had drained from his face, throwing the expression of anger and determination into stark contrast.

Despite his obvious discomfort, he didn't once ask Preston to slow down.

Preston had already disclosed everything he knew to the Sheriff, from the abductions leading up to Savannah's disappearance to the pattern he discovered in the children who went missing after her. He described the photographs taken of him while he investigated the Downey kidnapping, the snapshot of his daughter in front of his house, and the picture that had led him to Dandridge's house that very morning. In exchange, Dandridge detailed the horror of the clearing the professor and his students had discovered, the construction of the stone medicine wheel, the condition of the corpses committed to the cairns, and the computer disks exhumed from the ground. The Sheriff confirmed Preston's belief that the man who had orchestrated this whole thing had deliberately drawn them all into his web with the pictures he had sent to Preston and the university, but neither could divine the reason he would risk allowing them to close in on him when he had outmaneuvered them every step of the way. And the way Dandridge described the medicine wheel—a sadistic tableau of suffering—Preston was certain it had been meant to be found. But why? Was it possible they were dealing with a lunatic who simply craved infamy, his face on the cover of every newspaper across the country?

"How much farther?" Preston asked. The uneven road made his teeth chatter.

"Maybe five miles. Can you go any faster?"

"Not without killing us both."

"I'm willing to take that chance."

The Cherokee slid sideways through a turn before righting and accelerating through a trench formed by the encroaching wilderness.

"It could be nothing, but I noticed something odd on both of the videos," Dandridge said. "Did you see that strange reflection of light right at the end? Almost like a glare or a sunspot, coming from—"

"Savannah's chest," Preston finished for the Sheriff. "You saw the same thing on the other one?"

"Yeah, but for the life of me, I can't figure out what it is. I thought it was just a trick of the light in the first one. But two can't be a coincidence."

"It could have been a reflection of the overhead bulb or of a light mounted to the camera from the...blood. The shifting of the camera as the killer shut it off. I don't know." The trunks of the trees raced past to either side, packed together like cornstalks. "What I want to know is, what's the significance of the medicine wheel? Are we dealing with a crazy Indian making some sort of political statement or reenacting some ancient ritual?"

"I don't care who he is or why he did it. I just want my daughter back. And then I'd like nothing more than to tear him apart like he did to those children."

Preston didn't tell the Sheriff he would never get that opportunity. The man's life belonged to him, and *he* would be the one to end it in the manner of his choosing and over however long he decided to make the pain last. It was his right as a father, and the last thing he would ever be able to do for his baby girl.

Ten minutes passed in silence as they wended higher into the mountains and crossed through meadows where the road became little more than twin ruts in the tall grass. When they finally reached the terminus, Preston parked his car next to one of the police cruisers, a pine branch resting on his windshield. He stared across the impromptu parking lot toward where the trail led up the hillside. Over the crown of evergreens, sharp blue peaks cut the sky.

He killed the engine and hopped down to the dirt. Dandridge met him around the front of the car, and together they struck off toward the path.

Something wasn't right. He could feel it, an uncomfortable sensation of foreboding that caused the hackles on his shoulders and the base of his neck to stand painfully erect. The current in the air was almost electric, alive with potential.

"If we guess wrong and your daughter isn't here, we might as well be killing her ourselves," Preston said. He glanced at the Sheriff, whose hand already hovered anxiously over the grip of his pistol in its holster.

"She's up there somewhere," Dandridge said, breaking into a jog once they rounded the ERT van. "I can feel it."

But that didn't mean she was still alive. Preston sensed that his daughter was up there as well. He only hoped they hadn't met the same fate. In his mind, he saw a small dark room with cinder block walls and a bloodstained worktable. Was it possible that it was up here too, in some remote survivalist's cabin? The mental snapshot shifted, and the girl in the picture he had driven all the way from Colorado to save appeared on the table, bound in the same fashion as Savannah had been. A hideous shadow leaned over her from beside a tray of wicked implements and softly shushed her. Preston's jog became a sprint, and together he and the Sheriff hurtled through the forest toward the clearing where he would finally be reunited with what remained of his little girl.

VII

22 Miles West of Lander, Wyoming

Dandridge didn't know what he would do if anything happened to Maggie. Too much time had already elapsed. Even if they guessed right and the killer had brought her here, the window of opportunity had been more than long enough for the man to do whatever in the world he wanted to do to her. What kind of father did that make him? Unable to protect his daughter in his own home where she should have been safe and sound? Emotions warred inside of him—anger, fear, helplessness, panic. He could barely focus on the ground as the path rose and fell over the alternately rocky and eroded terrain. Every second that passed brought him closer to the clearing, but they were seconds he simply didn't have. He tripped and fell repeatedly, only to rise and stumble into a sprint again. His palms and knees bled, his chest ached from the exertion, and the physical reality had begun to set in. He was going to have to slow his pace to catch his breath or he was going to collapse.

Special Agent Preston lagged behind, but Dandridge could hear him huffing, struggling to stay close enough to maintain visual contact. Dandridge wasn't sure if he trusted the man. His appearance had been too well-timed, too convenient. However, he did feel a certain kinship to the man, who had lived through what he now endured. Assuming he was telling the truth. He believed everything the agent had told him so far—either that or he was one hell of an actor—but blind trust was a luxury he couldn't afford.

He fell again, only this time his trembling arms could barely push him up to all fours. Gasping for air, Preston caught up to him and helped haul him up. They both doubled over and sucked at the air as they walked.

"How much farther?" Preston panted.

"There's a valley just beyond that rise ahead. We're going to the top of the ridge on the other side. Maybe twenty minutes if we hurry."

"Then we're wasting time," the agent said, breaking into a jog.

When they reached the crest of the knoll, the agent suddenly ducked off the path and threw himself to the ground on his belly. Dandridge was just about to ask why when he saw movement at the bottom of the slope below them, the silhouette of a man moving through the trees toward the thin stream. The needled branches allowed fleeting glimpses of the man, only enough to determine that he was alone, until he emerged from the tree line into a meadow of thigh-high weeds at the edge of the stream.

"Grant," Dandridge said.

"The professor?" Preston rose and stared down at the man, who searched the bank for the narrowest section and hopped across. "What's he doing all the way out here?"

"I don't know, but I sure as hell intend to find out."

Together they picked their way down the steep, rocky trail, skidding on the loose gravel and bounding between rugged crags mountain goat-style. At the edge of the forest, they regained visual contact with the professor, who had begun to jog on a relatively level section of the path.

"Grant!" Dandridge called, his voice echoing through the valley.

The professor paused and turned in a slow circle, apparently unable to determine the direction from which Dandridge's voice had originated.

"Stay right there!" Dandridge ran through the slalom of pines and aspens, crossed the meadow at a sprint, and cleared the stream in a single leap. When he finally caught up with Grant, the relief on the professor's face was evident.

"Thank God," Grant gasped. "I was hoping I would run into someone before I made it all the way to the site. I've been trying to get a hold of you for hours now. Your dispatcher kept telling me she'd have someone call me back, but no one ever did and now I'm out of cell phone range—"

"What are you doing out here? You were supposed to stay at the motel until we were through with you."

"I had to tell someone, and since no one would return my calls, I figured that you were all still up here, so I decided to come out here in person and make you listen."

"Listen to what?" Dandridge asked. He tugged on the professor's arm to start him walking again.

"I think I know where the killer is."

VIII

The Sheriff stopped in his tracks and roughly turned him around. Les couldn't read the expression on the man's face: eyes wild, cheeks red, breathing ragged.

"Tell me!" Dandridge snapped, grabbing him by his shirt and nearly lifting him off the ground.

The other man, who looked out of place in a dirty suit, crooked tie, and sweat-stained shirt, pulled the Sheriff away from him and shoved them both ahead on the trail. No introduction had been made, nor did Les really care for one. All he wanted right now was to get out of this awful forest.

Les drew a deep breath as they scrabbled up the slope and told the men everything he had learned. He described the petroglyph, the smaller human renderings, the alignment of the celestial bodies, and the man rising from the pit. Until he actually heard the words coming out of his mouth, he didn't realize how insane he sounded. He half-expected them to openly mock him, or, based on their sour dispositions, toss him off the nearest cliff. Neither man reacted at first. They merely locked eyes and shared a silent conversation to which he wasn't privy. After a long moment, the Sheriff finally spoke.

"I want you to run, and I mean *run*, back to where the cars are parked. Get as far away from here as you possibly can."

"So you believe me?" Les asked.

The men made no reply. They drew their side arms and dashed away from him up the path.

Les didn't need to be told twice. He had delivered the warning as he had promised himself he would, and now, whatever happened, he could look at himself in the mirror with a clear conscience.

The men rounded the bend uphill and vanished into the forest, leaving only the sound of their scuffing footsteps in their wake.

For the first time in hours, Les breathed a sigh of relief. Granted, there was a part of him that wanted to further examine the medicine wheel, to be there when they found the man who had built it so he could learn its function, but the very last thing he wanted was to have to look into the eyes of a monster in the center of a ring composed of the bodies of murdered children.

He allowed himself a moment to revel in the sensation of the rising sun's caress on his face, and then started to run as he'd been instructed. Skidding down the steep path, he shouldered the tree trunks for leverage and eased around boulders until he reached the meadow, where he picked up his pace again. The golden grass wavered at the urging of the wind as he sprinted toward the stream, which was visible only as a dark line through the field. His right foot clipped something hidden by the weeds and he hit the ground shoulder-first. He rolled over and grabbed his ankle, from which pain radiated all the way up his shin, and shoved aside the tall grass to see what had tripped him.

A metallic flash of the reflected sun against tan fabric. Les recognized the badge on the deputy's chest before the man's face, which was smeared with blood. Lifeless blue eyes stared through him and into the heavens from bruised sockets. The nose was misshapen at the bridge, the lips split over broken teeth. The man's throat had been slit across the common carotids and trachea with such force that Les could see the hint of the cervical spine through the gaping laceration.

He gasped and scrambled in reverse, barely able to see over the feathered tips of the grass.

It was Deputy Henson, the same man who had driven him to the motel only hours earlier. The deputy must have returned here sometime afterward and been intercepted on his way back to the site.

Les surveyed the meadow around him. There was no sign of movement, save for the rolling waves of the amber grass and the shivering branches on the trees.

He was in the middle of nowhere and it was a long journey back to the cars, for which he didn't have a single key. The deputy—the *armed* deputy—hadn't even had enough warning to draw his pistol. And the body had been invisible in the weeds. He must have walked within inches of it just minutes ago. For all he knew, the man who had killed Henson could by lying in wait mere feet away. Or he could be anywhere for that matter.

Les eyed the trail that ascended the slope to the south and made a decision. He reached for Henson's utility belt and removed the gun with trembling hands.

If there was safety to be found, it would be in numbers. Especially well-armed numbers.

It was a long way back to the road, and he would be alone, separated from the others the entire way. At least in the opposite direction, there was a swarm of law enforcement officers who were undoubtedly much better trained with their weapons than he was.

Damn what the Sheriff said, he thought, and struck off cautiously to the north with a pistol he wasn't even certain he would be able to fire held out in his shaking grasp.

IX

Preston focused on the silence. They should have heard something by now. Voices. The clatter of stones. Anything. Dandridge had said they were nearly upon the clearing. So where was everybody? Suddenly, even the crunch of his own tread was too loud, his heavy breathing amplified. There was definitely something wrong.

An odd pine appeared at the side of the path, twisted, grotesque. Several paces ahead, an aspen had grown in the same corkscrew pattern.

"We're here," Dandridge whispered beside him. He too must have sensed that something was amiss.

Preston eased to the edge of the forest in a shooter's stance and surveyed the stone creation through the branches. More of those bizarre trees grew at random intervals. There was no one in the clearing. Nothing stirred, as though even the wind feared to enter the horrible scene spread out before him.

And then he saw the bodies. Skeletal remains wired in place as though to mock the innocence of the pose. Festering flesh. Bare bones. All in various stages of decomposition. The air was rank, the smell of death all around him, and beneath it, a faint, malodorous, yet almost sweet, scent. Preston recognized it immediately. Something had died here, and recently.

"Where are your men?" Preston whispered, leaning forward into a clump of scrub oak in hopes of gaining a better vantage.

Dandridge shook his head, apparently every bit as perplexed.

"How many officers should be here?"

"Seven," Dandridge whispered.

Preston nodded and pressed deeper into the branches. A wall of cold air struck him. It had to be several degrees cooler, even with the swatches of sunlight that lent the ground a checkered appearance. He tried not to look at what was left of the children, for he knew one of them was his little girl. His precious Savannah, the light of his life, who had been left at the mercy of the elements as though she had been worth nothing. He seethed, the pain and rage boiling in his bloodstream. It took all of his strength to hold back the scream of futility that welled in his chest. All of these children, all of these lives prematurely extinguished. The horrors their families had been forced to endure, and the sorrow that would be thrust upon them when they learned the fates of the sons and daughters for whom they had prayed and held out hope for so long.

Even as she was now, he wanted nothing more than to hold his daughter in his arms one last time. Let her know that she had mattered and that he'd never stopped looking for her. That she had been his world and he would have gladly taken her place. That he was sorry he hadn't been there when she had needed him most.

But first, he was going to find the monster who had done this, and he was going to inflict a measure of pain beyond the capacity of any human being to bear. Let them lock him away. With nothing left to live for, he no longer cared. He could deal with the consequences as long as he knew the killer would never hurt anyone again.

He turned to Dandridge and motioned for the Sheriff to circle around the east side while he rounded the clearing to the west. Dandridge gave a single nod, and, with the rustle of branches, vanished back into the woods.

Preston crept through the foliage, one eye on the dense forestation, the other on the medicine wheel to his right. It was just as the Sheriff had described it, only seeing it in person was much worse than he had imagined. The black stains of dissolution and the rust-colored crust of dried blood on the bones made them look tainted, as though the killer's evil had leeched into them even in death. He noted the stones were bereft of the lichen that would have grown on them over time. The dirt was a riot of footprints, and there were small patches between the uncovered remains and the central cairn where freshly-turned earth suggested that something had been recently buried. Was that where they had exhumed the disks, and, if so, had someone reburied them again? There were large sections of scuffed dirt toward the north and central portions of the clearing, possible signs of a struggle, and the telltale shallow trenches of something heavy being dragged away into the woods. He saw splotches and arcs of ebon mud, and there hadn't been any recent precipitation. There was no longer any question about what had happened to the Sheriff's men, but could one man have overcome seven trained law enforcement professionals or were they dealing with more than one killer?

He thought about what the professor had said, about the pit in the petroglyph. Was it possible the killer had simply risen from the ground in their midst and caught the officers by surprise? And was he preparing to do so again at this very moment? He pondered the idea that the children had been gathered posthumously to bear witness to some event beyond his comprehension, that twenty-eight—

Dandridge had said there were only twenty-seven corpses, and that there had been an obvious gap for the twenty-eighth, but he didn't see a break in the ring. Granted, the far side was hidden by the cluster of trees surrounding the central mound of stones...

He paused and counted the outer cairns, those both still intact and disassembled. There were definitely twenty-eight, which could mean only one thing.

They were too late.

Preston suddenly felt sick to his stomach. He glanced across the medicine wheel to where Dandridge darted through the trees like a specter, and was overcome by pity for what the man was about to experience.

A gentle breeze renewed the scent of fresh kill, guiding Preston farther to the north, toward where the dragging impressions in the dirt vanished into the forest. He passed the last of the partially-uncovered remains and reached the point where he had to lean closer in order to see the body inside through the gaps between the stones, hints of exposed bone, snarls of desiccated hair and skin.

His grip on his pistol grew slick, forcing him to readjust it, his finger firmly pressed on the trigger, eager for the opportunity to squeeze.

The smell intensified and the tracks in the dirt became more defined. Different treads and sizes, but whoever had dragged the bodies had been smart enough to use them to erase his tracks. The faint buzz of flies signaled that he was close.

Another dozen paces and he saw a heap of corpses in the alcove beneath a broad pine. Bloated flies spun lazily over a tangle of flesh. He quickly counted five faces, all covered with blood from matching cuts across their throats. Clean incisions. One swift stroke and the deed was done, surgical in its precision, deadly in its speed. It wouldn't have taken more than a matter of seconds for the men to bleed out, and none of them would have had a chance to call for help. These were methodical kills. The officers hadn't stumbled upon the killer, nor had they interrupted his work. These men had been hunted, their deaths precisely planned and executed. Almost as though they had been exactly where the killer had wanted them to be. Preston shuddered at the thought. Pictures had been sent to the right people to guarantee their presence at this site at exactly the right time, and whoever had orchestrated it had been ready, as though he had done this before.

There was no time to spare for the dead officers. Two were still unaccounted for, and if there was a chance they were still alive, however unlikely, they needed to be found. Or was it possible that one or both of them were in on the killings? That would explain how the other men had been so easily dispatched.

Too many questions. Too few answers.

He heard a strangled moan from the east and knew exactly what it meant.

Dandridge burst from the forest and ran toward one of the cairns. The ground surrounding it had been disturbed and then wiped clean by a pine branch, which left tiny needle scratches on the topsoil. Preston hurried after him, covering Dandridge along the barrel of his pistol. The Sheriff had holstered his weapon to free both hands so he could toss the rocks aside. He sobbed and moaned. Preston's heart ached for the man, but now was not the time to fall apart. The killer had enacted his plan with such meticulousness thus far that he was undoubtedly counting on the Sheriff's incapacitation.

"There's nothing you can do now," Preston said, jerking on Dandridge's collar.

"I need to know." He elbowed Preston, who absorbed the blow and pulled even harder. "I need to know if Maggie's in there."

"If she is, she's beyond our help."

"What if she's in there? What if she's still alive? Buried in there. Alone. Suffocating."

Preston knew there was no way anyone would have been able to prevent him from doing what Dandridge did now. He would have turned his weapon on whoever tried to stand in his way, with every intention of using it.

"Sheriff..." he whispered, and finally released the man's collar.

Rocks clattered behind him as he stood sentry, watching for the first hint of motion, hoping to put a round in the murderer's knee or his shoulder to buy them some quality time alone.

Dandridge bellowed into the sky. Preston turned around to find the Sheriff collapsed on his knees, not in front of the corpse he had expected to find, but before something else entirely. A dirty, stuffed bear lay on the dirt, covered with a mess of long blonde hair. Maggie's hair. That meant there was still a chance she might be alive if they could find her quickly enough.

Her abductor had known they would be here and had left these things so there would be no mistaking to whom they belonged. And, it was now apparent, the man who had taken her meant for the chase to continue.

Preston grabbed Dandridge around the chest and hauled him away from his daughter's belongings, his tortured cries echoing off into the forest.

X

Dandridge barely maintained some semblance of functionality. The moment he had seen Maggie's bear and all of that hair, the reality of the situation had set in and something ripped inside of him. The anger and indignation he had felt turned to fear, a sensation of helplessness so primal his body threatened to simply shut down. Whatever control he had thought he held was illusory. All of his training, his power, and his experience meant nothing. His daughter's life was in the hands of a twisted, sadistic demon for whom none of the normal rules seemed to apply, and there was nothing Dandridge could do to stop him.

At least Preston had had the presence of mind to draw his pistol for him and thrust it into his hand, where it now hung limply in his grasp. The agent shoved him toward the center of the clearing, all the while sweeping his sidearm in circles.

"Snap out of it!" Preston said. "I need you right now! Your daughter needs you!"

She's already dead, a voice said from the darkness in his mind. *There's nothing left for you now. You failed the one job that really mattered.*

"No," Dandridge whispered. No, he hadn't failed. Not yet. Until he saw Maggie's body with his own eyes, there was still hope, and he wasn't about to give up as long as there was even the slightest chance. His grip tightened on his pistol and the fugue began to clear. Rage pumped through his veins. If the man who had taken his child had meant to break him, then he had woefully underestimated his resolve.

His grinding teeth nipped the inside of his lip and he tasted blood, which only served to fuel his desire to see the monster's spilled as well.

He raised his weapon and scoured the tree line for any sign of movement, nerves flat-lined, arms steady.

"What do we do now?" he asked.

"We go down," Preston said as they reached the center cairn. He leaned over the edge and peered down into its depths. "Into the pit."

Dandridge scanned the forest one last time, then risked a quick glimpse into the cairn. The dirt on the bottom was sloppy with mud, a deep black stain with a spattered pattern around the edges. The inner rock walls still dripped with blood. He prayed it wasn't his daughter's as he scaled the stones and perched on the top. Nearly obscured by the shadows was a circular depression in the dirt, through which a dark seam coursed. The ring was too perfect for it to be natural. There was obviously something underneath.

"Cover me." He dropped down into the well. The soles of his boots met the earth with the hollow clang of a sewer drain lid that reverberated through the ground underfoot. "It's hollow," he called back up.

"Can you figure out how to get in?"

Dandridge kicked aside the mud and dirt to expose a rusted iron circle set into the ground. He searched for a hole he could use to lever it upward, tried to claw at seams too thin for him to curl his fingertips into.

"There's nothing to grab onto. No handle. No grips. No..." His voice trailed off. He dropped to his knees and brushed the blood-induced mud away from two small sections where there was no rust. They were textured differently from the rest of the iron cover. He pressed his palms over them and pushed down. Nothing happened. He tried turning it to the left. Nothing. When he twisted to the right, it turned with a grating sound until it reached a point where it suddenly dropped several inches, nearly causing him to fall forward. With a hydraulic hiss, the iron disc retreated into an underground recess.

Dandridge hopped up and braced his feet against the inner edges of the cairn as a dark maw opened under him. There was only darkness, a fathomless black tunnel that could have descended all the way to the Earth's core for all he could tell. But the smell...the smell that rushed up to greet him made him gag. He had once been party to legal proceedings that had led to the exhumation of a casket that had been buried three years earlier. The stench that had billowed out of that coffin when they opened it paled in comparison to this.

Using the stones for leverage, he lowered his right leg through the hole and tentatively swung it from side to side until he encountered resistance, then sought a solid foothold.

"There's something down here," he called up to where Preston was balanced on top of the cairn with his back to the pit, covering the surrounding clearing. Straining, Dandridge clambered sideways until he could lower his other foot down. He transferred his weight and cautiously pressed deeper. There was another rung about a foot down, and another below that. "It's a ladder, but I can't tell how far down it goes."

"Be careful," Preston said.

The Special Agent's warning fell on deaf ears as Dandridge descended the rungs, back pressed against the opposite side of the small tube. With each step, the stench intensified until his eyes watered and he retched repeatedly. The only sounds were the hollow tapping of his footfalls and the squeaking of his sweaty palms on the cold iron rungs.

If Maggie was down here, he was going to find her. And if anything had happened to her, he was going to avenge her.

Heart racing, legs trembling, he eased downward into the complete darkness of the tomb where the monster presumably waited with his baby girl.

A grim sense of foreboding passed through him, and with it came the certainty that only one of them, either he or the man he intended to kill, would ever see the light of day again.

Chapter Four

I

22 Miles West of Lander, Wyoming

With a final sweep of the medicine wheel, Preston tucked his pistol back into his holster and dropped into the pit. He lowered his right foot onto the top rung in the waiting darkness, then his left, and hurriedly clambered down into the black depths. He spared a single glance back toward the circle of sunlight as he plunged deeper. Somewhere below, the sounds of Dandridge's descent abated. A wan light rose from below him, highlighting the rungs just enough for him to hasten his pace. The outside world was all but invisible when the tunnel opened into a larger chamber and he stepped down onto a smooth stone floor.

Dandridge stood mere feet away, slowly illuminating the surrounding walls with his MagLite. Preston clicked on his penlight, drew his weapon, and aligned their sights. The smell was so awful he could hardly breathe. Is this where the man had brought his daughter? Had this horrible scent been the last thing she smelled? Had she contributed to it?

The room around them was square, perhaps fifteen feet to a side, each of which featured a lone dark opening leading away from them at the cardinal directions of the compass. Sloppily mortared cinder blocks reinforced the walls. The ceiling was reinforced with aged wood, through the slats of which something metallic glinted. It was a layer of corrugated aluminum, rusted to such a degree that he could see the bare stone through the gaping holes. No, not stone, but an ore of some kind, some sort of dense crystalline vein. The beam of his flashlight penetrated it slightly, suffusing it with a pale crimson glow.

"What is that?" Dandridge whispered.

Preston knew exactly what the Sheriff meant. The ground thrummed slightly underfoot. It almost felt as though his fillings were vibrating. He shook his head in response and tried to pry back the darkness that filled the doorways with his penlight.

"We split up," Preston whispered. "If you find anything, shout."

He didn't like the idea of exploring separately. They should have advanced into the darkness together, one covering the tunnel ahead, the other their rear. Alone they would be easier to pick off. The killer held every advantage here. But time was the most important factor. If Maggie wasn't already dead, then it was only a matter of time before she was.

Unspoken between them was the certainty that there was someone else down there with them. Preston felt it in the icy exhalations of the tunnels around him, like breath on his neck. He had seen the same realization in the Sheriff's eyes.

Dandridge nodded to his right and inched forward into the corridor, pistol and flashlight raised at arm's length.

Preston turned away and stepped into the black orifice before him. It was frightening how quickly his sense of direction had abandoned him to the darkness. The walls were bare, smooth stone, bracketed every few feet by rickety timber posts and cribs like an old mine shaft. Faded petroglyphs adorned the limestone, some smoothed to nothingness by time, others depicting an endless procession of stick figures and creatures from myth. Now was not the time to dwell upon them, for somewhere in the darkness, perhaps mere feet away, death lurked with a rusted scalpel.

The soft thrum became a mechanical shudder ahead.

His beam barely penetrated the darkness. He was beginning to feel as though the tunnel had no end when his light finally limned the terminal edges of the stone channel.

He stepped out into a room roughly the size of the first. A portable generator sputtered and coughed against the far wall, its exhaust vented into carbon-scored ductwork that led away along the ceiling to either side toward twin doorways. The small chamber smelled faintly of gasoline and diesel smoke, which barely managed to compete with the reek of decomposition. His beam played upon a single cord hanging overhead. He gave it a tug and the lone bulb bloomed from the cobwebs, casting a subdued brass glare over the room. There was a single mattress in the corner, dirty and stained with urine, the springs exposed in spots. Thick ropes were attached to eye rings in the concrete block wall, the entirety of which was stained nicotine yellow, except for the black corona around the generator. Aged bloodstains decorated the floor. The wall to his left showcased a collection of tattered clothes: dresses, pajamas, shirts and jeans…all hanging from rusted nails driven through the mortar between the bricks.

This was where he kept them. Before he took them to the room Preston was now convinced was somewhere in these catacombs. The nightmarish room from the videos where the shadow man ultimately killed them.

He had to look away, look at anything other than the soiled mattress where his daughter must have once been bound and the trophy wall of clothing where her birthday dress surely hung. In doing so, he noticed the cables and conduits running along the ceiling. They were caked with dust and grime, and alternately hidden by the rotting rafters and the swaying cobwebs. The copper conduits fanned out across the ceiling, a network of arteries leading away from the generator and into the dark tunnels that exited either side of the rear of the room at ninety-degree angles to the point at which he had entered.

Preston was contemplating whether or not he should follow one of the perpendicular channels or if he should return to the main hub when he heard commotion from down the corridor to his right, then a muffled curse.

He recognized Dandridge's voice. It sounded so far away…

The hair on the back of his arms rose electrically.

Slowly, silently, he aligned his penlight with his pistol and walked out of the room into another bare stone tunnel.

II

Dandridge pushed himself back to his feet. He had been so focused on everything around him that he hadn't been paying close enough attention to the ground. The cardboard box that had tripped him lay crushed in front of him, its contents scattered across the floor. There were packets of dehydrated rations in plain black and white packaging everywhere. They appeared to have been manufactured half a century ago. The flashlight confirmed that a good dozen more boxes contained the same payload. He turned the beam toward the wooden ceiling and caught the shadow of a string hanging in the middle of the room. A sharp tug summoned a weak glare from the exposed bulb. A cache of dusty bolt-action rifles and M16s lined the wall to his right, caked with dust and connected by cobwebs. Cases of ammunition were stacked beside them. Old wooden barrels dominated the rear wall between shadowed corridors leading to either side, their metal bands rusted to the point that they barely held the planks together, their circular lids no longer firmly seated.

It was a survivalist's den, possibly a bomb shelter assembled as the Cold War was beginning to ramp up. At a glance, he figured there were probably enough supplies for several people to hole up down here for many months, if not years. So where had they gone and why had none of them ever returned to at least reclaim their firearms?

He approached the nearest barrel and tipped back the lid, tearing away the spider webs the held it in place. Through white strands and funnels riddled with insect carcasses, he saw the hint of olive-green fatigues and manila bone. Skeletal remains had been crammed into the barrel in fetal position, the cranium fractured like an eggshell. He opened the next barrel, and the one after that. Each housed the decomposed corpse of a man—

Footsteps to his left.

He swung his pistol toward the sound. Preston materialized at the edge of his flashlight's reach, penlight and weapon pointed right back at him. Dandridge lowered his pistol and returned his attention to the chamber. A section of the bricked wall had been torn down and lay in rubble on the ground where the boxes of rations once must have been piled before being shoved awkwardly into the room. His beam spotlighted a wide oval of limestone conspicuously bereft of the layer of dust that clung to every other surface in the room. There was another petroglyph, similar to those carved into the walls of the tunnel that led here. He recognized it from the professor's description of its twin hundreds of miles away. Rows of smaller figures to either side of the mouth of a pit, at the bottom of which was a larger figure that was connected to another one in the sky by a series of wavy lines. There were stars and spirals, and other etchings that were much lighter, more recent additions. Geometric equations solved in angles and degrees, ratios and conversions taken out to several decimal places.

"The rooms are connected by rounded corridors I assume parallel the outer ring of the medicine wheel," Preston said. "The only thing in the room I just cleared was his wall of trophies."

"We need to keep moving," Dandridge said. His daughter was down here somewhere. Call it paternal instinct or even wishful thinking, but he was certain he could feel her nearby. And her silence scared the living hell out of him.

Together, they made their way back to the central chamber, which was now imbued with a soft rose hue. Through the slits in the wooden supports, the metallic ore glowed subtly. Was it a trick of his eyes after bumbling through the darkness...or something else?

He inclined his head toward the tunnel to the left to signal his intent and entered the mouth of the earthen orifice, leaving the Special Agent to explore the lone remaining branch. Slowing his pace, he scrutinized everything his cone of light passed over, prepared to pull the trigger at the first sign of movement.

They were down to two rooms. Either he or Preston were about to confront the man who had abducted their children and killed so many others.

A meek whimper from the darkness ahead.

Dandridge sprinted ahead, support timbers flashing past to either side in the shadows. A weak glow grew brighter ahead with each step until he could see the room beyond the end of the tunnel. He took in the details as quickly as he could. A stack of crates just across the threshold. A video camera on top. Past them, the sides of a wooden workbench. He couldn't see who was on the table, or if anyone even was, but if Maggie was lashed to that blood-crusted sheet of particle board, he had just run out of time.

He burst into the room and shoved aside the crates, which toppled to the floor and splintered with a loud crashing sound. The camera clattered away under the vile workbench. There was no one on the cutting surface. The rope bindings hung limply from the sides. His brow crinkled. He was sure he had heard—

A whimper from his right.

He turned toward its origin. A mound of filthy blankets was heaped in the corner. Something shuffled underneath them, just the slightest rustle. He threw himself to his knees in front of them, set down his pistol and light, and tossed the blankets aside as fast as he could. They were repulsive, stiff with urine, blood, and a host of other smells he couldn't identify. Hands trembling, breathing haggard, he struggled to uncover his daughter.

A meek mewling sound rose from under the last remaining blanket. He sobbed as he tore it away and revealed tangled blonde hair, dirty bare skin.

There was a loud *crack* he felt clear into the marrow of his bones. His vision swam. Warmth trickled down the back of his neck and under his collar. A throbbing pain gripped the base of his skull. He focused on the small pair of terrified blue eyes that stared up into his.

Maggie whined around the soiled sock that had been stuffed into her mouth and started to cry. She reached for him, but her wrists were lashed together.

He slumped forward and fell onto his daughter.

She clawed at his face, pulled his hair, tried to lift his head.

Her skin was warm against his cheek.

Whimpers that sounded as though they came from miles away followed him into the darkness.

III

Preston stood stock-still in the middle of the room. The entire scene was incongruous. A laptop computer rested on an ugly table fashioned from wooden scrap. Bloody handprints covered the casing as though the monster had been in such a hurry to review his work he hadn't even taken the time to wipe his hands on his pants. Cords led away from it in every direction. Power, inputs, outputs. A beating heart transplanted into a long-dead corpse. He should have expected as much, he knew, but for whatever reason he was still surprised. A laser printer rested on the floor beside boxes of blank DVDs and other memory storage devices. There were reams of unopened photo-quality printer paper and unopened ink cartridges.

He pulled the light switch and illuminated the otherwise barren space. The walls, however, were plastered with photographs. To his left, images printed from the laptop. They were hazy stills, snapshots stolen from the video feeds. Hundreds of them. Taped to the walls, to one another. An endless, seamless cavalcade of death. All children. He recognized their faces, for he had been hunting for each of them, some for as long as seven years. Only these weren't the smiling visages from the school pictures and the random snapshots. These were images of expressionless, dead children, his daughter among them. Bound to the table. Spatters and smears of blood on their faces and shoulders. Their glassy, partially-opened eyes windows into death.

Twenty-seven horizontal rows, one for each child.

Preston noticed that the children weren't the primary subject of the pictures. In each, a golden starburst like a blinding reflection, ill-defined and out-of-focus, bloomed from the chest of each victim. The images were aligned sequentially in a series separated by fractions of a second, depicting the ball of light as it swelled from a pinprick to the point that it nearly eclipsed the child's chest, and then diminished again to nothingness. He had seen the same thing in real-time on the recording that had been left for him at the Sheriff's house. Just a quick flash, a tilting mirror catching a reflection from the sun. Dandridge had seen it too, and had even commented that he had noticed it on one of the other videos.

What in the name of God was it, and how had the killer created it during the murders? Had there been someone else operating the camera while he performed his grisly act? Was it a trick of the lighting? A visual effect?

He turned and scrutinized the opposite wall, which was similarly covered with pictures. Only these weren't letter-size computer printouts. They were actual enlarged photographs, slightly grainy and yellowed. The camera's flash washed the subjects in an amber glare. More children. In a small room like the previous sets, only somewhere different. The walls weren't made of concrete blocks, but from packed earth from which serpentine roots protruded. There weren't numerous nearly identical pictures that could function as a flipbook that showed the genesis and dissipation of the hazy golden shape, but only two or three, the contrast blurry, making the children's faces appear smudged.

The rear of the chamber was similarly decorated, however the photographs were black and white, the edges curled and browned. Behind the subjects, the wall was constructed of smooth stones, stacked and mortared. A root cellar like the one at his grandmother's Colonial home in rural Virginia. There was only a single snapshot of the bright starburst, which nearly whitewashed the child's face.

Someone had done this same thing before. The historical account was all around him. Was he looking at the perpetuation of some sadistic experiment that began long before he was even born or a copycat mimicking the twisted wiles of a serial killer surely long since dead and buried?

And, again, what exactly was that strange reflection of light?

He was alone in the room and the sands were rapidly draining from the hourglass. He would have ample opportunity to thoroughly study the pictures and answer his questions later. Right now, there was still a little girl in grave danger, and he would be damned if he allowed her face to appear on the wall beside him.

The reality of the situation struck him like a fist to the gut.

They had now cleared three of the rooms, and if the killer was down there with them, he had to be hiding in one of the dark, rounded tunnels that connected the chambers, or he was in the last remaining room.

Where Dandridge was at this very second.

A moment's hesitation. He could either return to the central hub and advance through the main channel into the room, or he could take the most direct route and approach it from the rear. Neither option held the slightest appeal, but if the Sheriff had walked blindly into an ambush...

His decision made, Preston hurried into the tunnel that linked the two chambers from the back as fast as caution would allow. Even with his penlight, the darkness was smothering, the vertical posts supporting the earthen roof watchful sentries passing within inches of him. Someone could easily be hiding behind any one of them, pressed against the wall, and he wouldn't know until he was right on top of them.

A tingling feeling, like the sensation of an impending lightning strike, made every hair on his body stand on end.

Light reached into the tunnel from ahead, growing incrementally brighter as the passage curved toward the final remaining room. Were it even possible, the awful stench grew stronger. Through the arched opening, he saw the edge of a wooden worktable, heard a muffled whimper. Not in the voice of an adult, but in that of a child. A rope bound a tiny white wrist to the table.

Preston reached the end of the tunnel and flattened himself against the stone wall. His heart was beating so hard and fast that it caused his field of view to throb in time with his pulse. He heard scuffing footsteps, the clamor of metal wheels on the floor, and the clatter of surgical implements. A flood of warring emotions threatened to cripple him. He was terrified, but his rage superseded everything else. He wanted to see the man who had robbed him of his life and forced Savannah to suffer. The monster needed to have a face.

And then the monster needed to die.

Deep breath. In. Out.

Pistol steady, finger tight on the trigger.

He swung into the chamber and targeted the shadowed form leaning over the frightened child on the filthy table. The man pressed the tip of a scalpel gently into the girl's neck beside her trachea. She pinched her eyes shut and tried not to shake as she cried, for even that slight movement summoned a trickle of blood that rolled across her skin and dripped to the wooden surface.

"Welcome, Special Agent Preston," a scratchy, frail voice said. "You're just in time to watch her die."

IV

Les crouched at the edge of the clearing in a clump of junipers. He'd been watching for movement, listening for any sound, for what felt like an eternity. He had expected to find policemen crawling all over the site, excavating the entombed corpses and combing through the dirt, dusting for fingerprints, making casts of footprints, and snapping pictures from every conceivable angle. The last thing he had expected was to come upon the first twisted pine without having heard a single voice. Surely they were around here somewhere. After all, he couldn't have been more than ten or fifteen minutes behind the Sheriff and the man in the suit. So where had they gone?

His mind raced through the possibilities while he hid, barely able to see the exposed remains in front of him and the central cairn beyond through the emerald branches. The others must have discovered something important elsewhere in the woods. That had to be it. They were all gathered around some critical piece of evidence, or perhaps they had cornered the killer and were snapping cuffs on him at this very moment.

But he would have heard them. Situated on the top of this knoll with the sheer canyon to the west, the acoustics would have carried their voices across a significant distance.

His thoughts returned to the petroglyph. The small figures. The alignment of the stars and the sun on this very day. The spirals, the swirling vortices.

The larger figure of the man in the pit.

Les knew where the others had gone, but the prospect of following them terrified him.

There was no way he could go after them. Not down there. He couldn't even find the courage to set foot in the clearing. Who could blame him though? He wasn't a trained law enforcement officer. He wasn't even sure he would be able to fire the gun he had taken from the deputy's body if he had to. What was he supposed to do?

Turning around wasn't an option. He had already established as much. And there was no way he was going to wander off on his own in this forest where someone like Henson could be so easily overcome. That pretty much left doing exactly what he was doing now: cowering in a cluster of shrubs and waiting—

His vision wavered. No. It was the clearing itself. The air shimmered like heat rising from a desert highway, making the dirt appear almost fluid.

The ground beneath him trembled almost imperceptibly. Had it been doing so all this time and he had only just noticed it?

He craned his neck so he could see the sky. Through the snarled branches of the corkscrew pine, he saw the blazing sun rising into the tranquil blue. He had to shield his eyes against the glare. Ribbons of heat distorted the golden orb, which was now closer to this point on the Earth than at any other time of the year.

A faintly metallic taste filled his mouth.

An aspen leaf fell from one of the trees in front of him. It was snared by a momentary updraft before again descending, spinning as though trapped in a cyclone.

He caught motion from the corner of his eye, but when he turned, he saw only the decomposing remains of a posed child. The wind must have blown the young boy's straw-like hair. That had to be it. For a heartbeat, he thought he had seen the lifeless form shiver.

Suddenly, he didn't feel quite right. His body felt like a struck tuning fork, and every hair on his body rose electrically.

Something was definitely wrong here.

Was the dirt between the stacked stones of the medicine wheel a lighter shade of brown than it had been a moment ago?

He remembered the article he had read about the vortices in Sedona, Arizona. People claimed they experienced a preternatural sensation of calmness and relaxation in their proximity. What he felt now was the complete opposite.

More movement to his left.

When he glanced in that direction, he saw just the skeleton of a child, which shifted ever so slightly like a mirage.

His body tightened, as though every muscle cramped in unison. He needed to stretch, to yawn out the tension in his jaw.

He prayed this sensation wasn't a precursor to an acute attack of his MS.

Joints popping, he stood and stepped out from the underbrush. He was certain of it now. The ground was definitely vibrating. The topsoil appeared to be sifting itself and the detritus swirled on a breeze he couldn't feel.

He paused near the boy's carcass and reached tentatively toward it. His fingertips tingled and a static charge raised the hair on his head. The sensation diminished when he retracted his arm.

What in the name of God was happening here?

He picked his way across the clearing, slowly stepping over the rows of stones, which tapped and rattled. Turned earth marked the holes where the DVDs had been reburied. When he reached the central cairn, he climbed the spiraling trunk of a pine until he could lean over the top of the wall and peer into its depths. The mouth of a chute led downward into darkness, the sunlight behind him casting his shadow ten feet down the wall over a series of iron rungs.

A faint humming that reminded him of the sound of overhead power wires emanated from below.

He cupped his hand over his brow and glanced over his shoulder toward the rising sun, which had cleared the upper canopy of ponderosa pines. Soon it would reach its zenith, and, if he was correct, shine directly down the tube.

Les shivered at the thought.

What was going to happen when it did?

V

Preston sighted down the man's face, the details exaggerated by the dirty glow from the bulb. His eyes were recessed in shadow; the deep wrinkles in his forehead and cheeks a sharp contrast. Gray stubble. Sagging jowls. Ears with disproportionately large lobes. A tangled mane of greasy white hair. Hunched, bony shoulders. He wore a threadbare black suit that could have been stolen from the casket of a man buried a hundred years ago. It hung loosely on his cadaverous frame. He looked fragile, although he radiated a level of strength that belied his appearance.

"Drop the scalpel and back away from the girl," Preston said. It took every ounce of his restraint to keep from shooting the man in his twisted face. The last thing he wanted was for the scalpel to end up impaled in Maggie's throat.

The little girl whimpered and closed her eyes as tightly as she could. Preston willed her to find a safe place somewhere in her mind.

"Did you know that you can use a coat hanger to find a shallow grave?" the man asked, his voice like a rake across concrete. Preston couldn't see his eyes, but he could feel his stare crawling all over his skin, a swarm of mosquitoes searching for the weakest point from which to draw blood. "One of those metal ones. All you have to do is straighten it out and use it as you would a divining rod."

"Get that blade away from her neck—"

"You see, it's a little known fact, but as a body decomposes, it emits electromagnetic radiation, a faint signal not dissimilar to radio waves. The wire detects and aligns itself with the frequency so that it vibrates in time with harmonics that only it can hear." A horrible smile filled with black teeth, sharpened by decay, stretched the man's face. "And children, well...they're so full of potential they act like little capacitors."

Preston bared his teeth and fought against his rage. At this range, there was no chance he would miss the shot. He could put a bullet between the man's eyes with the slightest application of pressure on the trigger and paint the chamber in a spray of blood and gray matter before the body even registered its demise. But if the man's hand even twitched...

"Why do you think that is? Hmm?"

"I don't care why. Now get that scalpel away from her or so help me I'll—"

"Be responsible for her death. Now...put down your gun. You aren't going to shoot me. With a flick of the wrist, I can open her common carotid artery and she'll bleed to death in a matter of minutes. So do us both a favor and get that out of my face before it starts to make me nervous and my hands shake worse than they already do."

Again, the sickly smile of a corpse.

Preston kept his pistol targeted between those shadowed eyes.

The man shrugged and pressed deeper with the scalpel. Maggie screamed and bucked from the table. Blood swelled around the tip of the blade and dribbled down her neck, but fortunately there was no arterial spurt.

The warning received, Preston lowered his barrel to the man's chest.

"Why are you doing this?" he whispered.

"What you really want to know is why I killed *your* daughter. Isn't it obvious?" The man appeared genuinely disappointed when Preston didn't immediately reply. "Because I needed you to find me."

"That's why you sent me the pictures, the email? Because you wanted me to catch you?" Preston's face flushed with anger. "This is just a game to you? If you wanted me, there was no reason to involve Savannah. She was just a little girl! She never did anything to deserve this! None of them did!"

"Would you have searched as hard for me if she had been any other child?"

The pistol shook in Preston's grasp. A part of him no longer cared if the girl on the table lived or died. He wanted to kill this son of a bitch more than anything he had ever wanted in his entire life. It didn't matter what happened to him now. Everything of importance was gone. He had brought this suffering on his family. He was responsible for his daughter's painful, lonely death and for chasing away the love of his life. Shooting this monster was the only way he could begin to atone.

He raised his Beretta to the man's face again.

There was a grunt from somewhere on the ground to his left. He spared a quick glance. Dandridge was crumpled on the floor, hair matted with blood.

"We're the same, you know," the old man said. "We both hunt children."

The man smiled.

Preston bellowed in anguish. Tears streamed down his cheeks.

"Here's what you're going to do if you want this child set free," the man said, all traces of his former levity gone. "There is a rope on the ground to your left. You're going to use it to bind the girl's father's wrists behind his back. And I mean tight. Then you're going to remove his handcuffs from his belt and shackle yourself. If you try anything foolish, her blood with be on your hands."

"And then what? Neither of us will be able to defend her. You kill us, and then you kill her anyway. What's to stop you?"

"I give you my word that if you do as I say, I'll set the girl free."

"Your word means nothing to me. How many children have you killed already?"

"I lost count a long time ago." This time, the man's smile was almost wistful. "You have no leverage for negotiation. Either you do exactly what I tell you, or I bleed her right here and now."

The man slid the scalpel toward Maggie's chin for emphasis. She writhed and screamed through the dirty sock. Tears rolled from her eyes. The first drop of blood dripped to the floor from the edge of the table.

"You do, and I promise you will suffer like no man has ever suffered before."

A garbled sound from his left.

Preston refused to break eye contact with the old man, fearing what would happen if he did.

"Please," Dandridge repeated, the word slurred. "Please...do it."

"He'll kill all of us," Preston snapped.

"My daughter...I don't care what happens..." He spat out a mouthful of blood. "...happens to me. But Maggie...if she dies, I die with her anyway."

Preston looked quickly at the Sheriff, who pleaded with his eyes. Were their situations reversed, Preston knew he would have wanted the exact same thing. When all that remains is hope, relinquishing it is fatal.

"The rope is on the floor between the two of you."

Preston couldn't bear to look at the man any longer. That awful smile made him ill.

"Are you sure?" Preston asked. "If I do this, neither of us will be able to protect her."

"If there's a chance...for Maggie, I need...need to take it."

"He's going to kill her regardless."

"What would you do...if it was your daughter?"

Preston closed his eyes for a long second, then slowly lowered his pistol. He didn't need to see the man to know that the smile had widened. It radiated a coldness he could feel even from across the room. He holstered his Beretta and walked toward Dandridge, detached, as though moving through a dream. The rope lay at his feet, frayed and crisp with dried blood. He picked it up and knelt behind the Sheriff, who had rolled onto his belly and positioned his hands behind his waist.

"Handcuff yourself first," the man said.

"Buy how am I supposed to tie—?"

"Bind them in front of you. You'll still be able to work the rope into a knot."

Preston removed the cuffs from the Sheriff's belt and clicked them around his wrists. The finality of the sound brought with it the reality that he was never leaving this mountain.

"I'm sorry," Dandridge whispered.

"So am I."

Preston looped the rope around the Sheriff's wrists and tied it tight, hoping he had left just enough wiggle room that Dandridge could shed them in a pinch, but not so much that the man would immediately notice and vent his frustrations on the child.

"All right," Preston said, turning toward the worktable. "I did what you asked, now let the girl—"

The man was no longer there.

Maggie had turned her head to face him, teary eyes wide, panicked. She shrieked through her gag.

Preston's stomach dropped.

Maggie wasn't looking at him.

She was looking behind him.

He heard a whistle of air, then a *crack*.

An explosion of pain from the back of his head, a metallic taste in his sinuses.

He toppled forward toward Dandridge, unable to raise his arms to break his fall.

Blackness claimed him before he landed on the prone Sheriff's back.

VI

Dandridge grunted and strained to scoot out from under Preston's weight. A pair of dirty, callused feet passed in front of him, hooked yellow nails like talons, a vast network of bulging veins. The cuffs of the man's pants were ragged and crusted. A blunt wooden mallet dangled from his grasp, dripping blood. It fell from the man's withered hand as he passed and clattered to the ground inches from Dandridge's face. There was hair crusted into the congealed blood on the flattened end.

He wormed away and tried to prop himself on his side, but the way he was bound made it nearly impossible.

Pressure on his wrists. His arms were jerked behind him with nearly enough force to dislocate his shoulders. Something slithered beneath his bindings. Another rope was tied around the first. He tugged to no avail. Comprehension dawned and the ground dropped out from beneath him.

He was now secured to the wall.

There was a scraping sound from somewhere out of sight. He craned his neck as far as it would go and caught a glimpse of the man restacking the crates he had toppled in his hurry to reach his daughter. The man rounded them, leaned under the edge of the table, and slid his camcorder back out where he could reach it.

Dandridge's head throbbed. He was certain he could feel his blood pumping in time with his pulse out of what felt like a crater in his skull. A wave of dizziness nearly made him vomit. Even thinking hurt. He was so groggy that his thoughts had become disconnected, threads unraveling faster than he could grab the ends. His eyes closed of their own volition, but he managed to force them open again.

The man now stood behind the crates. He set the camera on the top crate, snapped out the small viewing screen, and tilted the camcorder so that it faced the table where his daughter shuddered as she cried. A tiny red light bloomed from above the lens and there was a soft whirring noise. He held a small chalkboard in front of the camera.

"No," Dandridge whimpered. "Please, God. You promised..."

The man made no reply. He merely set down the chalkboard and walked around to the other side of the table toward Maggie.

She sobbed and shook her head from side to side, strained against her bindings.

Dandridge struggled to his knees and threw himself forward, but the ropes held fast. He worked his wrists back and forth, the braid tearing through his skin. Blood trickled into his palms, and still he jerked. His shoulders popped and it felt like he might de-glove the flesh on his hands.

"Don't do this. Let her go. Do whatever you want to me. Just don't hurt her. Don't hurt my daughter."

The man tilted his head and offered a tight-lipped, placating smile, not without an element of sympathy, and lifted the scalpel from where he had set it down on the blood-crusted particle board beside Maggie.

"No!" Dandridge shouted. "We did what you wanted! You said you wouldn't hurt her! You promised to let her go!"

The man sighed and slowly rolled his eyes to meet Dandridge's.

"I said I'd set her free. I never once said anything about letting her live."

Dandridge bellowed and hurled himself away from the wall. Over and over. Joints cracked. Bones snapped. Skin tore. Blood flowed freely from his wrists. He screamed and thrashed. Begged. Pleaded. Cursed. Vowed. Right up until the moment the man opened his baby girl's neck with a flick of his wrist.

A hollow gasp, and the crying ceased.

A whistle of air.

A gurgling sound.

Dandridge collapsed to his knees in tears. From the corner of his eye, he saw a strobe of golden light, and Maggie's small, naked body fell still on the table. He lolled onto his side and sobbed.

He heard the patter of fluid on the ground, as though someone had left a faucet running.

Bare feet crossed in front of him again and he lunged for them, trying to trip them with his shoulder, to latch onto them with his teeth. He was going to kill this man if he had to rip off his own arms to do it.

The man stooped, grabbed Preston by the shirt collar, and dragged him toward the doorway, trailing a wet smear in his wake.

"I'll give you a moment to say goodbye," the man said, and with that, pulled the unconscious agent into the dark tunnel, leaving Dandridge alone with his pain and his sorrow...and the lifeless body of his daughter.

VII

Les resisted the urge to call down the tube, and instead paced around the central cairn, careful not to trip over the short walls that formed the spokes of the wagon wheel design or step in any of the blood. What in the name of God was he doing here anyway? He wanted to run away, yet the prospect of being alone in the woods with a killer who was intimately more familiar with them than he was frightened him. But if the man who had done all of this was down there, somewhere underground, then walking away would be the safest thing he could do. However, if there was more than one man involved, his theory fell apart. At least out in the open, he would be able to see anyone approaching with enough advance warning to get a head start. Of course, that also left him uncomfortably exposed.

He simply didn't know what to do, so he continued to pace and hoped the right choice would present itself.

The sun cast strange and shifting shadows from the twisted trees onto the shivering ground as it neared its zenith. The air around him wavered as though the earth had begun to bake. There had to be some outside force stronger than the sun's rays acting upon the clearing, but for the life of him, he couldn't imagine what.

He looked heavenward again and noticed something he hadn't seen before. Nearly hidden by the branches over the stone well was a web of ropes a shade lighter than the bark. They'd been strung between the upper reaches of the trees in a crisscrossing fashion. He had to climb up onto the stones to clearly see them. Several black carabiners hung in the middle.

A metallic clang rose from the hole beneath him.

He gasped and leapt down from the stone ring.

Someone was climbing up the ladder.

It was probably the Sheriff and the other man, but he couldn't afford to take the chance. Everything about the situation felt wrong. Why had there been no voices preceding the sound of footsteps on the rungs?

He stumbled when he hit the ground, righted himself, and sprinted toward the forest. Behind him, the sound faded to nothingness, and was replaced by a humming noise that seemed to originate from both inside of him and all around him at once. It coincided with the vibrations underfoot, as though his body somehow conducted it. Hurdling stones and rounding the rotting remains of a young boy, he plunged into the underbrush and flattened himself to the dirt. He could barely see into the clearing through a clump of wild grasses and the overhanging branches of scrub oak. After a moment, a head emerged from the well, followed by a pair of stooped shoulders.

Les closed his hand over his mouth and focused on slowing his breathing.

It wasn't the Sheriff or the man in the suit, or any sort of officer for that matter. The man was far older. From this distance, he appeared to be well into his seventies, and yet he moved like a man half his age. He had greasy white hair and a black suit jacket so filthy it could have been peeled off a recently disinterred corpse. There was no physical way this man could be the killer, but if he wasn't, then who in the world was he and what was he doing here?

Les unconsciously shrunk back into the shrub.

The old man climbed up onto the top of the ring of stones, took a moment to steady himself, and then stood up. He reached into the needled canopy. In his right hand, he held a long rope, similar to those strung through the branches. He struggled with something for nearly a minute, both hands working out of sight, and then jumped to the ground, still holding the rope, which angled up into the trees, and then straight down into the hole. He must have run it through the carabiners.

The ground vibrated with such urgency under Les's chest that he was certain it affected the electrical impulses in his heart, its very beat. His watch shifted on his wrist, the hasp opening of its own accord.

Slinging the rope over his shoulder, the old man grasped it in both hands and walked away from the central cairn. His face clenched with the exertion. He was hauling something up the tunnel, something heavy. When he reached the outer ring of cairns, no more than fifteen feet diagonally to Les's right, he kicked aside a stone to expose a metal eye ring staked into the dirt. With obvious difficulty, the old man fed the end of the cord through the hole and then continued to tug. His eyes bulged and he bared his decayed teeth with the exertion. He abruptly turned toward the middle of the clearing.

Les followed his gaze and watched in horror as a pair of bound hands rose over the lip of the cairn, followed by a pair of arms wearing a suit jacket, and then a head, which nodded limply against a white Henley and loosened tie. The man's shirt was covered in blood, his hair wet with it. He continued to rise until his entire torso was up in the branches, leaving only his legs hanging over the hole, twirling in slow circles.

It was the same man he had met in the forest with the Sheriff less than an hour ago.

If he was here, then where was the Sheriff?

The old man groaned as he tied off the end of the rope. He gave it a sharp tug to test its strength. With a satisfied nod, he ran his fingers along the length of the rope as he returned to the trees from which the man now hung.

Les felt his keys shift in his pocket.

When he reached the central cairn, the old man glanced over his shoulder.

Les closed his eyes and pressed himself into the dirt. He was sure that the old man had looked directly at him through rheumy, cataract-blotched eyes. Les forced his lids open just in time to see the crown of white hair vanish down the mouth of the well.

He listened for the sound of footsteps on the iron rungs, but heard only the humming in his head.

If he made a break for it now, there was no way the old man would be able to catch him. Les was no world-class athlete, but he felt confident he could outrun the hunched man. However, they had all underestimated the old man, and if he'd been able to overcome all of the police that had been here, then Les might not prove as much of a challenge as he thought.

And then there was the man strung up in the trees. His body wavered through the ribbons of heat as thought roasting over an open fire in the pit. He couldn't just leave him there, could he?

His mind shoved forth an image of the petroglyph. He envisioned the larger man in the sky connected to the one in the bottom of the pit by a series of squiggly lines.

He had no idea what was about to happen, but the sinking sensation in his gut told him he didn't want to find out. The air around him was alive, positively crackling with energy.

Les pushed himself up to all fours and crawled cautiously out into the clearing.

He needed to get the man down.

VIII

Dandridge stared at the lifeless body on the table in front of him. Maggie's skin continued to pale before his eyes, passing from stark white to translucence. Bruises blossomed through the smeared dirt and the spatters of blood. The pain was more than he could bear. He wanted to die, to escape the torture by any means possible. He had failed in the only responsibility that had mattered, and now his baby girl was dead.

His moans and sobs echoed back at him in the confines and haunted the tunnels leading deeper into the warren, but he no longer heard them.

In his mind, he was holding his swaddled child to his chest. Margaret had been so red and wrinkled, her tiny hand barely able to wrap around his index finger. He remembered that she had kept her eyes closed against the light, that her lips had quivered then she cried, exposing bare rows of gums. He remembered holding this tiny, fragile part of him in his arms and vowing that he would never let anything happen to her, that he would protect her from the world and its evils.

And now the only thing he wanted was to free her from her bindings, cradle her in his arms one last time, and beg God to transfer his life force into her. Or else allow him to follow her into the grave.

He no longer deserved to live. He had forfeited that right.

An image of his wife's face rose unbidden. He saw pain and anguish beyond anything she had ever experienced, and he saw the blame in her eyes. Even as she sat at home, waiting by the phone for him to call, he knew he had killed her as well.

A distant, hollow series of clanging sounds reached his ears, followed by scuffing footsteps.

Anger boiled inside of him, his thoughts a burbling cauldron of incoherence. He lusted for blood. He was going to kill this man with his bare hands. He was going to subject him to pain beyond the capacity of human suffering. He was going to strip him of his black soul and send him straight to hell.

The footsteps grew louder until the old man stepped into the bronze glow from the dark channel.

Dandridge roared and lunged at him, over and over, no longer feeling the strain in his shoulders and wrists, the blood flowing over his hands.

The man paid him no heed. He simply removed the video recorder from the top crate, tucked it into his jacket pocket, and walked over to the end of the workbench. One by one, he untied the ropes that bound Maggie's wrists and ankles, and let them fall away from the particle board. As though she were nothing more than a sack of grain, he hefted her from the table and slung her over his shoulder.

"Leave her alone!" Dandridge shouted. "Don't take her from me again! I'll kill you! No matter where you go, I will find you, and I will destroy you!"

"You will try," the man said with a sigh, and cast a forlorn glance over his shoulder as he entered the tunnel. Maggie's long blonde hair and limp arms swayed against his back.

And then he was gone.

Dandridge bellowed so loud it felt like his throat tore. He braced his feet and pushed away from the wall with everything he had. His shoulders cracked, but remained seated in the joints. The rope cut off the last of the feeling in his hands, and still he couldn't pull them through the knot.

The footsteps faded into the resultant silence and he screamed in agony.

There was no way he was going to allow his daughter to be wrapped in barbed wire and posed like the others, to be violated even more in death.

He turned and studied the wall behind him. The rope was secured to a rusted eye bolt with a knot the size of his fist. He scanned the floor for anything he could use to cut it. The only possibility was his pistol, but even if he managed to reach it and maneuver it into firing position behind his back, there was no way he would be able to shoot with any kind of accuracy.

Again, he focused on the eye bolt.

He walked toward it and studied it closely. There was a small gap in the ring around the rope. It just might be wide enough...

Turning around, Dandridge grappled with the knot until he was able to force his thumbs down into the eye bolt. He wedged them in there all the way past the base, until he knew they wouldn't be able to slip out too soon.

An odd calmness rippled through him. He became acutely aware of the current in the air, of the trembling ground beneath his feet, of the static electricity that raised the fine hairs all over his body. Of the pain that was soon to come.

He drew a deep breath, steadied his shaking legs, and fell forward to his knees.

The bones in his thumbs snapped with a resounding *crack*. Pain raced up his arms and into his shoulders, where it burned, white hot, in the torn cartilage.

He screamed and fought to retain consciousness, while his body simply wanted to shut down.

Using his fingers, he folded his bloody, broken thumbs into his palms and threw himself forward. The bindings snagged on his wrists. He drove himself away from the wall, pushing harder and harder, until the rope fell away and he slammed into the table. The particle board fractured under his weight. He slid on the wet surface, his daughter's cold lifeblood soaking into his clothing, and collapsed to the floor.

Dandridge held out his mangled hands and evaluated the damage. His thumbs protruded at obscene angles. Streams of blood drained into his palms from the lacerated skin. Getting them back into their sockets was going to be a bitch, but he didn't have time to screw around. He flattened his left hand on the ground, formed an awkward fist with his right, and aligned it with his crooked left thumb. His struck it with all his might and bellowed as he slammed it back into the socket. It hurt even more now, but when he flexed it, at least he could see it respond. Encouraged, he repeated the process on his right thumb, then hurried back across the chamber to where his Px4 Storm lay, and lifted it from the dirt floor.

It took a moment to find a solid grip with the ferocious pain in his thumb.

Holding the pistol in front of him, he crept into the shadowed tunnel, heart racing in anticipation of the kill.

Chapter Five

I

22 Miles West of Lander, Wyoming

The pain roused Preston. He felt like he'd been hit by a truck. His first thought was a splash of ice-cold water in the face.

The Sheriff's daughter was dead.

Those five words brought clarity to his shattered thoughts and cut through the humming sound in his head. He opened his eyes a crack, but the light was too bright, staining his vision scarlet. The sun beat down on him, burning his scalp. Blood trickled along his neck from the source of the searing pain. He tried to wipe it away, but his hands were unresponsive. He had no feeling in either upper extremity. He could barely breathe with the way his shoulders pressed against his head and neck. With a groan, he spat out a mouthful of blood and tried to open his eyes again.

The world of red resolved into a forest of green. There were pine needles everywhere. He tried to turn his head, but only managed to twirl in a slow circle. Raising his head summoned a fresh stream of warmth from the wound on the base of his skull and an explosion of pain that nearly chased him back into unconsciousness. He swung his feet in hopes of finding purchase, but found none. Calling for help only produced a dry rasp that stung his throat.

Slowly, the details around him came into focus. He was handcuffed with his arms above his head, secured to the trees. Below his dangling feet, which throbbed with the accumulation of blood, he saw the ring of stones that formed the cairn in the center of the medicine wheel. Somewhere down there was the hole leading into the series of chambers, but he couldn't quite see it.

The ground surrounding him wavered like a desert mirage, surely a symptom of the concussion the blow to his head must have caused.

He attempted to pull himself upward in an effort to evaluate the mechanism by which he was suspended, tried to wrench his hands out of the cuffs, but nothing worked.

A shape darted into view below him. It took his eyes a moment to track it. The professor climbed up onto the rock ledge, swayed until he found his balance, and grabbed him around the legs. He wrapped Preston's knees to his chest and lifted.

"Can you reach the metal clips holding the rope?" Dr. Grant whispered.

Preston willed his numb fingers to move. After several attempts, he shook his head.

"Try harder. We don't have much time. He could come back at any second."

Preston strained against the cuffs, but his best efforts barely made his fingers twitch.

A hollow tapping sound echoed from far below.

The professor looked up at him, a wide-eyed expression of sheer terror on his pale face. He released Preston's legs, leapt from the cairn, and sprinted out of sight.

"Wait..." Preston rasped. His newfound momentum caused him to swing around again.

The tapping noise grew louder and louder. He heard heavy breathing, the clatter of stones, and then the old man appeared, the naked body of Maggie Dandridge draped over his shoulder.

Preston sagged and nearly drifted off into unconsciousness again. There was no longer any doubt in his mind that the little girl was dead. He had never stood a chance of saving her. The old man had been in control every step of the way. All that remained now was to die himself. Undoubtedly, the Sheriff had already been killed, and the professor was probably running for dear life into the forest. That left him alone, strung up like a deer waiting to be gutted.

It was all over now. A part of him resigned to his impending demise, while the rest of him became incensed at the thought of losing his one opportunity to avenge his daughter.

The cuffs ratcheted tighter on his wrists. His gun tugged against its holster and his keys shifted in the pocket of his pants.

He started to turn in circles, but he had made no movement and felt no breeze.

Several minutes passed, during which the dizziness caused him to drift in and out of awareness. The old man reappeared below him, scaling the short wall. That awful wrinkled face looked up at him and flashed a foul grin, then, with a wink, the man descended into the darkness. His clanging footsteps eventually faded into silence.

Needles shivered loose from the branches surrounding Preston and spiraled toward the ground.

The air around him rippled.

He tasted metal in his mouth.

Pressure mounted in his sinuses, which released a trickle of blood from his nose with a loud *snap*.

Droplets swelled from his lips and chin, fell away, and swirled down toward the cairn.

II

As soon as the old man was out of sight, Les raced back out into the clearing and straight toward where the man in the suit hung. He had nearly abandoned the man to his fate when the old man emerged with the corpse of the young girl, but after watching the care with which the monster had brushed her hair from her face and posed her almost like a Precious Moments figurine, he had reached the conclusion that if he left now, he wouldn't be able to live with himself. There was something truly evil about the old man that went beyond the act of killing the children. The old man needed to die, but he certainly wasn't the one to do it. He had zero skill with a gun and couldn't even determine of the blasted pistol had a safety or not. Surely the Sheriff was already dead, which left the man suspended above him as his last hope.

The stones shivered as he climbed the wall. He struggled to find any sort of balance until he again grabbed the man's legs.

"I can't find anything to cut the rope," he said, hoping the man could hear him over the humming sound, which seemed to intensify with each passing minute. He didn't dare speak any louder. "So I'm going to try to pull you down. Maybe our combined weight will be more than the rope or the carabiners can support."

He glanced down into the mouth of the pit. The sunlight stretched nearly to the bottom now, casting both of their shadows clear down the cement chute to the point where he could vaguely discern the circular outlet of the tunnel and the bottom of the iron ladder.

There wasn't much time left before the sun aligned as it did in the petroglyph. Maybe nothing would happen, but with the way the ground shuddered and appeared to radiate heat that he couldn't feel, he wasn't willing to take that chance.

He hugged the man's knees and jerked, tugged, pulled.

The man groaned in pain above him.

Les couldn't afford to stop now. The earth trembled. The air shimmered. Even his vision shivered.

One of the flat stones wiggled loose and toppled out from under him. He fell forward, grasping the man's slacks to keep from falling.

A shout from above him as their amassed weight was transferred to the man's wrists.

With a *snap*, one of the ropes that formed the network in the trees split and dropped them several inches.

Les slid down the man's legs and clung to his ankles, arms tight around his shoes.

He looked into the tunnel directly beneath him, no more than four feet down. If he fell, it would take some serious acrobatics to keep from plummeting straight down the chute. A figure stepped into view far below. The sunlight caught his wrinkled face and their eyes met across the distance. A momentary expression of confusion crossed the old man's features, and then he smiled.

Les felt a surge of panic and tried to swing his legs back to the rock wall.

The old man raised his arms out to his sides as the sunlight enveloped him.

Les turned away. Golden stars appeared in front of the cairns in the outer ring, rising from the patches of turned earth where the DVDs were buried. The bodies of the uncovered children shook and almost appeared to raise their heads toward the blossoms of light.

His belt buckle pulled him downward.

His keys tugged against his pocket.

The force was too great. His arms slipped and he grabbed for anything within reach.

Blazing light below.

The golden sunspots around him, now circling around the cairn in tightening spirals.

Dead children, shaking, trembling.

Intense pressure in his head, a sensation of displacement, of something reaching inside of him and forcing out his every conscious thought.

Laughter in his ears, originating from the core of his being.

A smile on his lips.

He tasted blood, felt warmth pour over his chin.

Another rope snapped overhead, dropping them with a lurch.

His arms closed around nothing but air and he watched the pair of shoes rise above him against the blinding glare of the sun.

Falling.

Weightless.

Les was swallowed by darkness as he plummeted down into the tunnel.

III

Preston felt the ropes release him, and then he was falling. He caught flashes of movement all around him as the ground rushed up toward him. Small stars, like the sun reflecting from so many shards from a shattered mirror, rising from the earth and swirling around him. Movement throughout the clearing, stones tumbling away from the cairns, the bodies already exposed trembling and raising their desiccated faces to the heavens.

His torso flopped forward and he caught just a glimpse of Grant's face before the professor vanished into the tunnel, staring directly into his eyes, reaching for him. There was no fear in his expression, no panic. Only a smile that appeared wider than his face could accommodate. A golden reflection from his eyes, and Grant was gone.

Preston's chest struck the ring of stones, knocking the wind out of him. Ribs cracked. Pain exploded through his whole body. He barely managed to grab onto the rocks and dragged himself over the rim just enough to keep from toppling backward into the hole.

The stone wall collapsed and toppled outward. Preston slid down the cascade of stones and struck his head.

He pushed himself to all fours, blood flowing from the gash across his hairline, barely able to gasp for breath through the searing pain in his chest, and crawled over the mound of stones to the hole.

Arms throbbing, the returned circulation flowing like lava through his veins, he eased down into the chute, found a tenuous grip on the iron ladder, and began his arduous descent.

IV

Dandridge staggered toward the end of the tunnel and the main chamber beyond. A blinding light forced him to shield his eyes. The old man was silhouetted in the heart of the glare, arms raised to his sides, back arched, staring upward with his mouth open in a soundless scream.

The Sheriff leveled his pistol with the man's knee.

Before he could squeeze the trigger, a dark shape appeared from above the old man and slammed him to the ground. There was a loud *crack* like a board breaking. A tangle of bodies rested on the floor in front of him.

Still. Unmoving.

Dandridge crept closer, weapon trained on the shadowed forms in the brilliant column of light.

One of them started to cry.

"Where am I?" a meek voice sobbed. "I'm not supposed to be here."

As Dandridge neared, the intensity of the sunlight waned and details came into focus. The professor was crumpled on top of the old man, the back of his head resting on that filthy suit jacket. Grant's knees stood from the ground at severe angles, his fractured fibulae poking out through his flesh, his tibias bent sharply. His eyes were closed. Dandridge couldn't confirm that the professor had survived the fall until he was close enough to see the subtle rise and fall of Grant's chest.

The crying intensified, filled with pain, fear, sorrow.

Dandridge felt no sympathy. He stared down into the old man's face. Tears rolled through the wrinkles on his cheeks from milky white eyes. His shoulders shuddered, making the ends of the broken clavicles that had ripped through his jacket twitch.

"How did I get here?" the old man moaned. He pawed tentatively at the sharp bones protruding from his upper chest and turned to face Dandridge. "Help me. Please. Please help me…"

The Sheriff leaned over, grabbed the old man by the collar of his jacket, and dragged him out from beneath the professor, whose head fell to the ground with the *clack* of teeth. He hauled the old man up and dropped him to his knees.

The old man fell forward and caught himself with his arms before his face could hit the ground. He screamed in pain and sobbed even harder.

"Look at me," Dandridge said.

The old man hung his head like a beaten dog, his whole body shaking.

"I said look at me!" Dandridge pressed the barrel of his pistol against the bone protruding from the old man's jacket. Hard. He wailed and raised his eyes to meet the Sheriff's.

"I don't know why I'm here," the man whimpered.

Dandridge grabbed a fistful of the man's hair, jerked his head back, and shoved the barrel into his right eye. He heard an irregular clattering sound and looked up to see Preston struggling down the ladder. Their stares locked for a long moment.

The old man cried and tried to pull away, but Dandridge pulled his hair even harder to hold him in place.

An understanding passed between the agent and him. Preston released his stare with a lone, slow nod.

Dandridge looked back at the old man. He committed the expression of fear on that sagging face to memory.

"I don't know why I'm here," the old man whined again.

Dandridge pulled the trigger. The crown of the old man's skull came away in his grasp with a handful of hair and scalp. Blood splashed across the floor and drained from walls pocked with chunks of bone and spongy gray matter. The body toppled awkwardly backward, legs crumpled beneath it.

A cloud of cordite smoke hung in the air.

The gun fell from his hand with a clatter.

Dandridge shambled across the room. He barely glanced at Preston as he shouldered past and started up the ladder on numb arms and legs.

The ground now barely shivered. By the time he reached the top, it was completely still.

He climbed out of the hole under the baking sun, clambered over the fallen rock wall, and crossed the clearing.

In his mind, he saw a beautiful twelve year-old girl kneeling on the ground, hair like spun gold blowing in the breeze. She smiled up at him and he took her in his arms for the last time.

Barbed wire tearing his uniform shirt, gashing his skin, he cradled his daughter's lifeless body to his chest, and cried softly into her neck.

V

Preston studied the ruined corpse at his feet. It looked so frail, so weak. A wave of repulsion, of unadulterated hatred washed over him. In his final moments, the old man had cried like the children he had slaughtered without remorse. He hadn't defied his fate with his final breath. There had been no epithets. Only a meek, pathetic old man who preyed on children because they were weaker than he was, because they were helpless against him.

With a bellow of rage, Preston raised his heel and drove it down onto what little remained of the man's face. Over and over. Bones snapped. Blood dripped from his foot. The dead face became a bruised and bloody pulp. A smoldering paste poured out of the exit wound.

Everything he had worked for, everything he had sacrificed over the last six years to bring him to this place in time…and now it was over. This monster would never hurt another soul again. It was of little solace, however. His daughter was still gone, and she would never be coming back. She had died down here. In the darkness. In pain. His name on her lips. His Savannah, the light of his life, had called the only name that had ever truly mattered to him on her dying breaths.

Daddy…

He closed his eyes and imagined he could sense her presence with him, smell her, hear the precious sound of her voice.

She was free now. As he knew that she would want him to be as well.

Preston turned away from what was left of the old man.

The professor groaned and attempted to sit up.

"Don't try to move," Preston said. He walked around the mess, knelt beside Grant, and placed a hand on the professor's chest to dissuade him from rising. "Just try to relax. We'll find a way to get you out of here, but you won't be walking on those legs for a while."

Grant moaned and rolled his head to the side. He stared at the carnage for a long moment. Preston was sure he saw the ghost of a smile on the professor's face before Grant again looked up at the ceiling and closed his eyes.

Preston clapped the professor on the shoulder in silent thanks, and started back up the ladder toward the clearing, where the solstice sun shined down on the shattered remains of his broken heart, and on the daughter to whom he could finally bring peace.

Chapter Six

I

June 22nd

22 Miles West of Lander, Wyoming

By the time the sun set, the clearing was again crawling with law enforcement officers. The FBI had airlifted in portable generators and enough sodium halide domes to light up a football field. Cords duct taped into bundles the size of Preston's arm ran everywhere. They snaked through the forest, along the stone spokes of the medicine wheel, and down into the hole, from which a column of light shone up into the night sky. Field agents from every available government agency sifted through the aftermath of the day's ordeal. Nearly the entire staff of forensics investigators had been flown in from the Bureau office in Denver.

Preston could only stare in awe at the intricately choreographed dance.

All of the stones had been unstacked from the outer cairns and meticulously tagged, photographed, and dusted. The bodies inside had been laid bare and photographed. It turned out the barbed wire that had bound them was a single continuous piece, run between the cairns under the outer ring of stones. They had unraveled it, divided it into sections, and tagged it with the victim number that corresponded to the body it had been wrapped around. The remains had been bagged and now rested off to the side where they awaited thorough evaluation by a team of medical examiners who were prepared to drop their current case load and devote their full attention to the children, whose remains, after being missing for so long, would need to be returned to their families, who would now have to mourn the loss of their sons and daughters.

Preston knew how they would feel, for he had already spent the majority of the afternoon saying goodbye to what little was left of his baby girl. He had always hoped that finding her would bring a measure of closure, to at least allow the wounds to begin to heal, but the hole in his heart remained. He now knew the pain would never pass.

What kind of person would that make him if he allowed it to?

Dandridge had spent the better part of the evening consoling his wife, who now rested comfortably in a pharmaceutically-induced sleep under the watchful eyes of the physicians at Lander Regional Hospital, where Dr. Lester Grant would soon be placed in recovery following the orthopedic surgery that had replaced his tibial shafts with titanium rods. Preston owed the man a debt of gratitude. At some point, he was going to have to swing by the hospital and express his thanks. It was the least he could do for the man who could have left him strung up in the trees for Lord only knew what to happen.

That's why he was still here.

There were too many unanswered questions. He needed to know what the killer had expected to happen, and he needed to be able to rationalize what he had felt and seen. The glowing lights, the mirror-like reflections without visible sources. The humming sound. The magnetic pull that had affected his keys, his pistol, even his fillings. He needed to know why the killer had told him about the electromagnetic properties of the decomposing children, if that was even true. But most of all, he had to know why. Why had his daughter been stolen from him, and why had she needed to die?

He looked over to where Dandridge stood at the edge of the clearing with a blank expression on his face, staring somewhere in the middle distance. Both of his hands were in splints. Preston hadn't seen him return. After everything they had been through, the Sheriff should have stayed with his wife, where he could console her, and, in turn, allow himself to be consoled. Preston envied him that luxury. Soon enough he would have to tell Jessie, who would close the door on him and seek comfort in the arms of her new husband and continue to live through her new child. His obsession to find Savannah had consumed so much of his being that it was all he knew now. Without the hunt, what was he supposed to do? There was no life left for him to resume.

Dandridge acknowledged him with a slight nod. Preston walked over to where the Sheriff stood and surveyed the scene at his side. He cradled his aching chest. His entire torso had been wrapped with tape under his shirt to ease the pressure on his fractured ribs.

Together they watched a group of agents in navy and gold FBI windbreakers raise a body bag from the mouth of the tube where the central cairn had once stood.

"His name was Walter Louis Cochran," Dandridge said, inclining his head toward the black vinyl bag. "They had just ID'd him when I arrived. Seventy-two years old. Left his wife in 1976. Not a word from him since." He paused. "Want to hear the kicker?"

Preston nodded. Where had the old man been hiding for more than three decades, and why had he chosen to resurface like…this?

"He was a homicide detective in Edmonton. Punched out one day. Never punched in the next. They found the body of his ten year-old stepson two days later."

"So how did he end up here?" Preston whispered.

He walked between the short stone walls toward where the other agents were gathered around the earthen orifice, Dandridge at his heel. A familiar face caught his eye. The Bureau was pulling out all the stops on this one before it became a media circus. Marshall Dolan, the thirty-something Assistant Director of the Rocky Mountain Regional Computer Forensics Laboratory, the shared forensics arm of the FBI and the Denver Police Department, glanced in his direction. Marshall had been kind enough to allow him to search the missing persons databases pretty much at will following Savannah's abduction, and had not only donated hours of his personal time, but had been instrumental in helping Preston formulate the theory that had led him to the pattern he had found in the kidnappings.

Marshall offered a sympathetic nod and removed his non-latex gloves to shake hands.

"You can't imagine how sorry I am that it played out like this," he said. "I was really hoping it would be different, you know?"

Preston thanked him, and pulled him off to the side, out of earshot from the other agents. Dandridge hovered nearby, listening attentively, feigning distraction.

"What did you guys find down there?" Preston asked.

Marshall looked him squarely in the eyes.

"You've already been through a lot today, and the coming days won't be much kinder. Are you sure you really want to know?"

"I *have* to know, Marshall."

"This stays between us." Marshall glanced over his shoulder in the direction of the other agents. "You got that?"

"Yeah."

Marshall nodded, and, with obvious reluctance, started in little more than a whisper.

"First of all, there's a tunnel that branches from the northeast corridor and leads to what passes for a road about a mile away in a shallow valley. We believe that's how he brought in the victim and was able to sneak up on the officers whose bodies we found in the forest. There's a rusted, unregistered El Camino parked under a screen of pines."

"What about the whole medicine wheel design?"

"I hesitate to wager a guess just yet, but you know how it was built over those underground tunnels? Turns out that's an old bomb shelter down there. Built by a bunch of Korean War vets back in the Sixties. We identified them by the dog tags we found on the corpses we pulled out of those barrels. It doesn't appear as though anyone ever missed them, sadly enough. Anyway, the caves obviously predate the construction. These guys just reinforced them structurally in hopes of withstanding a nuclear assault. They also added the generator to supply the electricity, reinforced the chute with concrete, and installed the iron ladder. Here's where it gets interesting. They ran the electrical cables through copper conduits in a complete circle around the central chamber, from which smaller cords branched off to supply all of the other rooms. They also ran the electricity up the tube to power the hydraulic seal and provide surface access. Remember what's at the center? That iron ladder. What happens when you run an electrical current—especially thirty amps at two-hundred forty volts—around an iron core?" He waited for Preston to take the next logical step. Preston only shrugged. "You create an electromagnet. Granted, there weren't enough coils around the ladder, nor were they in close enough proximity to make an especially powerful one, but that would probably explain what you said you felt. And the humming sound as well."

"The old man said something about the bodies of the children giving off electromagnetic radiation as they decomposed."

"Well, sure, but with a wavelength so long you'd basically have to be right on top of them to even detect it."

"Would the barbed wire conduct it?"

"Theoretically, but we're still talking about the corpses producing an infinitesimally small current that could barely generate a measurable magnetic field." Marshall scoffed, but checked himself when he saw the expression of frustration on Preston's face. "Look. Say the bodies produced a small electromagnetic field, and the generator below created a much larger one, the only reason two fields of varying strength would be significant is if you're trying to create some sort of primitive, exceptionally low-energy particle accelerator. Even then, one of the magnetic fields would need to be flipped, or polarized, to accelerate electrons toward a target. And what would be the purpose of that? There's no source of electrons, no target, and no reason to waste any more time or effort contemplating this. I know you're trying to come up with some way to justify why this happened, trying to rationalize your daughter's death. I hate to be so blunt, but I think you're just going to have to chalk it up to the sick and twisted fantasies of a psychopath. You know as well as I do that there are deranged people out there that are simply monsters without consciences. They do terrible things, which, no matter how you look at them, never make sense." He rested a hand on Preston's shoulder and looked him directly in the eyes. "I won't pretend to know how you must feel, but I'm telling you, as a friend, you're going to have to deal with this in a way that allows you to move on."

Preston nodded and averted his eyes. He understood what Marshall was saying, and appreciated the sentiment, however he knew there was no way he would ever be able to let it go. Not without swallowing a bullet.

Marshall clapped him on the shoulder and turned to rejoin his team.

"One more quick question," Preston called after him.

Marshall favored him with an impatient smile.

"The lights I saw, when I was hanging from the trees. They looked like reflections, only they were several feet in the air."

"That one I can answer definitively. You ever heard of a *glory*?"

Preston shook his head.

"It's an optical illusion. A trick of light. The ground here has a high concentration of calcite sand, not to mention the dense crystalline formation directly above the underground structure. You see, calcite has unique optical properties. Basically, a light wave enters a calcite crystal from one side, becomes polarized, and breaks into two different waves. Kind of like a reflection from the windshield of a car. And, viola…You have yourself a spectral apparition."

"You said something earlier about polarization in regard to the magnetic field…"

"You're grasping at straws, Preston." Marshall gave a half-hearted wave and struck off toward the others. "And if there's one day in the year when you might expect some strange tricks of light, today would be that day."

Preston's brow furrowed.

"The Summer Solstice," he whispered and turned to Dandridge, whose expression matched his own.

II

June 23rd

Laramie, Wyoming

Dandridge stood on the porch of the bungalow two blocks from the main campus. He had driven east to Laramie on a hunch, and he knew better than to ignore his hunches. From where he stood, he could see the University of Wyoming, a sprawling collection of salmon-colored brick buildings connected by underground passages that allowed the students to keep from freezing to death in the winter at the hands of the wicked winds. Dandridge pressed the doorbell and waited. The only car in front of the house was his Blazer, and the neighborhood itself seemed to be holding its breath, waiting for the students to return for the fall semester. He rang again and listened. No sound of footsteps or the creak of floorboards. He glanced again toward the street, opened the screen door, and tested the front door knob. It turned easily in his hand.

He wished he could pin down what was bothering him well enough to vocalize it. Maybe tying off a loose end was an oversimplification. Perhaps that was all he would end up doing, but his gut told him otherwise.

Yesterday, the day following the ordeal at the medicine wheel, had been spent in one interrogation after another. Each of the interviewers had asked the same questions on behalf of a different agency, and he had given the exact same answers each and every time. He had barely been able to return home in time to arrange for his daughter's burial, which would unfortunately have to wait until

after the autopsy by the medical examiner and the official release
of her remains from the FBI. The delay worked out well. He didn't
want to hold Maggie's funeral while his wife was still hospitalized
and under psychiatric care. The doctors were confident of her
prognosis and expected to release her within the next couple of
days, once they figured out the proper dosages of the dozens of
pills she would have to take. One of the shrinks had offered to refer
him to a colleague so he could talk about how *he* felt, but
Dandridge had politely declined. He knew exactly how he felt.
Even though he had shot the old man in the face, something deep
down insisted that the case was far from closed.

After visiting his wife this morning—sitting in a chair at her
bedside and watching her lapse in and out of drug-fueled
catatonia—he had sprung for a box of overpriced chocolates at the
gift shop and wandered down the hall to check on the professor.
He had found Grant's room empty, the linens bunched at the foot
of the bed, the wardrobe bare, save for a crumpled hospital gown.
The charge nurse had been genuinely surprised when he asked
where the professor had gone. Grant hadn't even been cleared to
leave his bed to use the bathroom with assistance, let alone attempt
to bear weight. The sutures in his legs were too fresh, the bones
nowhere near healed. A quick search of the wing had proven a
waste of time. It wasn't until they widened their search to include
the entire facility that a cafeteria worker reported that she had seen
a man in a wheelchair rolling himself out the front doors toward a
waiting taxi.

There had been no previous discussion of discharge against
medical advice, nor had Grant been anything other than the model
patient. He had simply changed into the clothes they had cut off of
him in the emergency room, gathered his few belongings, and
slipped out without a word.

Dandridge hadn't known the man long, but this impetuousness
didn't fit with his established behavior patterns. Thus, when a call
placed to the taxi service had revealed a destination of Laramie,
Dandridge had volunteered to follow up himself. He was still the
Sheriff after all.

A call to the university had confirmed what he suspected.
Grant hadn't been in contact and his office was locked up tight.
That meant he had to have gone home, but as Dandridge opened

the door and stepped into the sparsely-furnished living room, he knew Grant had already come and gone.

"Dr. Grant?" he called.

The empty house swallowed his words.

A wheelchair lay overturned on the floor beside a pile of clothing, including the pair of jeans that had been cut to mid-thigh to gain access to the compound fractures. He turned right down the main hallway. Droplets of blood spotted the carpet. He passed a bathroom on his left, a study on his right, and entered the master bedroom at the end. Several garments were strewn across the bed. Drawers stood open, their contents hanging over the lips. The closet door was ajar, hangers scattered on the floor, shirts and pants crumpled beneath the rails where they had once hung. There was a floor safe in the corner, door wide open, empty inside. A scrap of paper with the combination was on the floor beside it, folded and worn as though it had been inside a wallet for a long time.

Where had the professor run off to in such a hurry?

Dandridge was confident he would find him soon enough.

The real question was why?

He glanced at the kitchen on his way back to the living room. The refrigerator door was open, the inner light splayed on the linoleum. Cupboard doors hung wide. A box of cereal rested on its side, raisins and flakes everywhere.

A cordless phone had been cast aside onto the couch. He picked it up and hit the redial button.

"'Lo?" a young man's voice answered.

"This is Fremont County Sheriff Keith Dandridge. With whom am I speaking?"

There was a long pause. Dandridge imagined the kid running through recent events to determine if he was in the clear of whatever he had done that he probably shouldn't have.

"Eric Wright, sir."

"Mr. Wright, can you tell me why someone would have called your house from this number?"

"You're calling from Dr. Grant's house, right? I have it on Caller ID. My roommate's in several of his classes. Lane Thomas. He left about half an hour ago. Said he needed to do a quick favor for Dr. Grant."

"Do you know what that favor was?"

"Yeah. Sure. He said the professor needed a ride over to the health center on campus since his legs were all busted up or something."

"And that's where your roommate is now?"

"I don't know. It's not like I'm his mom or anything. He doesn't need to run all his plans past me."

"Can you give me Mr. Thomas's cell phone number?"

Dandridge committed it to memory and hurried back out to his Blazer, already dialing as he peeled away from the curb. Lane answered on the third ring and corroborated what his roommate had told him. He had picked Grant up roughly half an hour prior and dropped him off at the Student Health Center with a duffel bag stuffed so full it looked like Grant anticipated staying for several weeks. Lane said Grant could barely walk and had to bite his lip against the pain with every step. By the time he hung up, Dandridge had pulled into the parking lot behind the clinic.

He ran through the door and surprised the receptionist, who sat at a desk beside a triage nurse. The nurse was currently occupied with a kid who wore a hat that showcased his Greek letters low across his brow in an effort to hide his obviously broken nose.

"Did a man named Lester Grant check in with you?" he nearly shouted.

"Sir. I'm sure you understand that patient privacy is regulated by HIPAA—"

"Yes or no? Or do I cuff you for obstruction?"

It was a bluff, but with the way her eyes widened, she didn't know it. She scanned through the list of registrants with a manicured fingernail, looked back up at him, and shook her head.

"Damn it," Dandridge said, rushing back out to his car.

He leapt into the driver's seat, grabbed his radio, and, even though he had yet to formulate solid justification as to why, prepared to put out an APB on Grant.

Something caught his eye and his heart skipped a beat.

The radio fell from his hand and clattered to the console.

He slowly climbed out and walked across the parking lot.

There was a bench with the beaming face of a real estate agent on the street beyond.

A pole with a bright blue sign stood beside it. On the sign was the letter A. The bus route.

Dandridge glanced down.

Several dark droplets of blood dotted the sidewalk. He dabbed one with a fingertip.

Still damp.

If there had been cash in the safe in Grant's closet, they were never going to find him. He could have gotten off at any stop, boarded any transfer, or simply gone straight to the Greyhound station. He could be on a bus to anywhere in the country at this very moment, or he could be holed up in a motel under an alias. All Dandridge could hope was that someone had noticed a man who must have been walking with great difficulty, a pained expression on his face, leaving a trail of blood behind him. But by the time they tracked down someone who remembered seeing him, too much time would have elapsed.

He returned to his Blazer to go through the motions, hoping to get lucky, all the while wondering what had gotten into the professor's head to make him run.

III

June 27th

Evergreen, Colorado

Preston sat at his kitchen table, laptop open before him. He planned to make good use of the time off the Bureau had forced upon him. Two paid weeks to get his life in order, grieve his loss, and return ready to work once more. He had initially resisted. After all, what did he have to do? The only pursuit that had kept him going was now gone.

And then he had received the call from Sheriff Dandridge, and suddenly he knew there was still much work left to be done.

Dandridge had just arrived. He paced the kitchen, rubbing his weary eyes. Like Preston, he hadn't had more than a few uninterrupted hours of sleep in a single stretch during the last week. Maybe it was the sleep deprivation or a shared delusion, but both of them were convinced that even though Cochran was dead, the evil was still out there somewhere, and Grant was the key to finding it.

Preston had yet to take off the suit he had worn to Savannah's funeral that morning. Despite everything leading up to it, the service had been beautiful. His baby girl had finally been laid to rest in a small white casket on top of a forested knoll overlooking a thin stream lined with aspens. A marble angel knelt above her grave, the pedestal that supported it engraved with the epitaph *Let thy child rest in hope and rise in glory*. He had purchased the adjacent plot, and smiled at the thought of being reunited with her sometime soon.

But first, there was something he needed to do. For her. For himself. For the children he felt, deep down, would one day need his help.

"Any news about Grant?" Preston asked.

"We lost his trail at the Greyhound station in Cheyenne. We found several eyewitnesses who remember seeing him, but none of them saw him board a bus or noted his destination. Since he paid in cash, we don't even have a credit card trail to follow. There were a dozen different busses departing during the timeframe we pieced together, heading in any number of directions. I'd wager he hopped a bus to Denver since it was the closest destination. From there he could have transferred to another cross-country bus or skipped over to the airport. He could be anywhere in the world by now."

Preston nodded. The professor's sudden flight didn't sit well with him either. His most vivid memory of the man was the expression on his face as he fell away into the waiting mouth of the tunnel. There had been no fear in that expression. In fact, Preston was almost certain Grant had smiled. He had witnessed the same momentary expression when the professor had seen the old man's corpse on the ground beside him. Had Grant not bolted without explanation, Preston probably never would have even remembered, but now that he did, those mental images haunted him.

"And what did you find that was so important that you couldn't just tell me over the phone? This wasn't the best time to drive down here, you know. My wife's been a wreck since Maggie's funeral yesterday, and the docs have her so doped up that she hasn't even gotten out of bed since." He poured himself a cup of coffee, sat down beside Preston, and sighed. "Sorry. I don't think I'm dealing with all of this very well either. There's a part of me that can't let it go. Heck. Grant probably just wanted to get away from everything so he could recuperate in peace. The guy potentially saved both of our lives, and here I am, prepared to track him to the ends of the earth based on nothing more than a gut instinct. Maybe I'm having a breakdown like everyone seems to think."

"Then it must be contagious," Preston said. He opened the manila folder beside his laptop, pulled out a stack of printouts, and slapped them down on the table in front of the Sheriff.

"What are these?"

"Copies of the photographs that were pinned up on the walls in the southern chamber of the bomb shelter."

"They look like they were taken a hundred years ago."

"More like seventy, actually. The top six photographs were taken between 1939 and 1941." He moused through a string of menus until he opened a screen that contained rows of thumbnail images. Double-clicking the first one brought up a black and white picture of a row of dead children lined shoulder-to-shoulder on canvas tarps in a progression of decomposition, from the nearly skeletal remains on the left to a young boy on the right who looked like he could have just been sleeping. "This picture was taken on June 25th, 1942. The children were found displayed just like you see them now in Montana, about fifteen miles south of the Canadian border in Glacier National Park. "Now if you look at the victims individually, you'll see they don't have any traits in common. Different eye color. Different hair length and color. Totally different age, facial structure, and body types. The only similarity is in the pictures in front of you. Each of those photos was taken at the time of death, and each has that optical illusion Marshall called a glory."

"But didn't he say it was the sun that caused them? These were obviously taken inside in a dark room."

"Caused by the flash, they speculate."

"Who did they make for the killer?"

"There was never a collar, but a Flathead County Sheriff's Deputy named Frank Johnson, who was investigating three of the abductions, including the kidnapping of his own nine year-old daughter, disappeared around the same time they found the bodies. Coincidentally, a drifter washed up on the shore of the Whitefish River two weeks later. They were never able to ID him based on how long he had been in the water and the damage caused by the local wildlife."

"And they never did find Johnson?"

"Actually..." Preston held up a finger to signify he needed a minute, closed out the screen, and opened another. "He did eventually turn up. Or rather, his body did anyway. Thirty-three years later and across the Canadian border. By the side of Highway 40 outside of Edmonton. A single gunshot wound to the back of the head. Execution-style."

"Edmonton?" The Sheriff's eyes flashed with recognition. "Cochran was an officer in Edmonton."

"Exactly." Preston opened the first thumbnail image. "The discovery of Johnson's body was overshadowed by this." He gestured to the screen. "They found the children just like this three days prior."

The picture showed a small clearing ringed by evergreens. Dead children hung by their necks from the canopy, heads lolled to the side, naked, bare feet pointing at the dirt. Wires connected them through the branches in what at first appeared to be a sadistic mockery of a carousel. A circular trench had been carved into the earth below them, above the top of which a series of corroded car batteries stood, connected by jumper cables. A metal pole had been planted in the center, the rusted, T-shaped post of an old clothesline. The trunks of the trees from which the children dangled had grown in spirals. And on the ground, small, flat stones had been arranged in a medicine wheel design

Preston waited for Dandridge to comment, but the Sheriff only furrowed his brow and delved into the copies of the photographs.

"There are twelve of them this time," Dandridge said. "Six. Twelve. Twenty-eight. An obvious escalation."

"And again, each of those photos was taken at the time of death."

"And all of them have that reflection."

"What are the chances of catching it in every single picture?"

"Unless the killer was somehow creating it, the odds against it have to be astronomical."

"Precisely."

"What are you suggesting?"

Preston paused to formulate his words. He needed Dandridge to reach the same conclusion that he had, and it definitely wasn't the kind of thing that could be spoon-fed.

"The connection between these two cases and ours is undeniable. And there's an element of escalation, but there's also an evolution of the methodology. The killer is refining his work as he goes. Hung children become posed. Car batteries are supplanted by a gas generator. Thirty-five millimeter film gives way to digital video. As I think that the manner in which the killer presents the scene has become more brazen, almost as though he's showing off, flaunting his crimes since he knows there's nothing we can do to stop him. With the murders in Montana seventy years ago, the killer had to have removed the bodies from the scene and laid them out somewhere different. That was the last time he felt any sort of fear of the consequences."

"Then the killers are somehow connected. There's no way one person could have done them all. Cochran was in his seventies. He would have been a toddler when the first set of victims was found. No. We're dealing with multiple murderers here. They knew each other, or at least knew of each other's work. They're trying to improve upon a common theme, to one-up the killer who came before them, or at least put their personal stamp on it."

"You're missing the key factor."

"That they were law enforcement officers assigned to the previous case?"

"Right. Johnson is investigating the abductions in Flathead County. He disappears around the same time the remains of the children are found and an unknown drifter is pulled out of the Whitefish River. He turns up dead more than thirty years later at the same time the police discover the children hung from the trees. And then Cochran, one of the officers involved, vanishes, only to reappear here, another thirty-some years later, the indisputable murderer of twenty-eight children. He now has only half of his face. Do you see the pattern?"

"By that logic, one of us should have disappeared."

"One of us did. Just not either of us."

"Grant?"

"It fits the pattern."

Dandridge scoffed. "You and I both know the professor is incapable of killing anybody."

"You didn't see his expression when he fell into the pit, and then again when he saw Cochran's body. It was the smile. The same smile I saw on Cochran's face when he was still alive. The more I think about it, the more I realize that Grant wasn't supposed to be there. His function was to lead us there, but he should have stayed at the motel. All of the other officers who had been there had their throats slit. It should have just been the two of us."

"So what are you saying?"

"Remember the petroglyph Grant told us about?" Preston switched to a different screen, which showed the picture taken from the rock in Banff National Park side-by-side with the one on the wall in the underground warren. They were nearly identical. "Both were carved at the same time, roughly a thousand years ago. And they both depict the exact same event. Smaller figures underneath an alignment of stars corresponding to the Summer Solstice. A larger figure in the pit below connected by wavy lines to another suspended above. That was me. Cochran was trying to recreate the scene from the petroglyph, only I don't think he anticipated Grant would end up hanging from my legs when everything started to happen, making him the closest to the tunnel."

"You need to get some sleep. You aren't making any sense."

"Think about it. After the professor fell on Cochran, you were alone with him. You talked to him. You looked him in the eyes before you shot him. You heard what he said, how he said it. Tell me he was the same man that killed your daughter. Tell me his mannerisms were the same. His voice. His expressions. Tell me that when you looked into his eyes you saw the same monster inside."

Preston brought up an image of Cochran's lifeless body sprawled on the ground, a mess of blood surrounding the ruin of his head.

"Tell me he was the same person."

IV

Dandridge rose from the table and paced the room. In his mind, he relived the last minutes of Cochran's life for the thousandth time. Grant plummeting down onto the old man. Dragging Cochran out from under the professor and to his knees. The old man whining and crying.

How did I get here?

The trembling hands, the expression of fear he had not once seen on the face of the demon that had killed his child. Those eyes. They had appeared to age, to reflect an inner confusion. The way Cochran pawed so pathetically at his fractured clavicle.

Help me. Please. Please help me…

"He took a hard blow to the head," Dandridge said, more to himself than to Preston. "A concussion can alter mannerisms, speech patterns, induce confusion."

Preston merely stared at him without speaking a word.

Dandridge ransacked his memory.

The mixed expression of surprise and terror on the old man's face when he shoved the barrel of the pistol into his eye. The way he had shrunken back, tried to look away.

I don't know why I'm here.

The old man had neither begged for his life nor hurled epithets. There had been no gloating as Dandridge would have expected. No bargaining. No struggle. There hadn't even been acquiescence.

Only confusion.

And every reaction suggested that Cochran wasn't faking it.

I don't know why I'm here.

Dandridge relived the kick of the weapon in his hand, the warmth on his skin. The faintly sulfurous smell of gunpowder. The explosion of blood and cranial matter. The body slumping to the ground at his feet.

He remembered Marshall's words from the following day, about the bodies generating a small magnetic field above the ground and the generator producing a much larger one below.

The only reason two fields of varying strength would be significant is if you're trying to create some sort of primitive, low-energy particle accelerator. Even then, one of the two magnetic fields would have to be flipped, or polarized, to accelerate electrons toward a target.

The larger stick figure above the pit on the petroglyph. Preston strung up by his wrists.

The figure below, the old man who had defiantly killed his daughter before his very eyes. A different man than the one who had cowered on his knees before the bullet removed the majority of his skull.

There's no source of electrons, no target...

But there had been, hadn't there?

A murderer who had once been a police officer who had disappeared during the investigation of similar killings.

The federal agent who would follow him to the ends of the earth to learn his daughter's fate and avenge her.

Dandridge recalled what Marshall had said about the strange lights Preston had seen, the very same optical illusions that had been caught on film over the chests of each and every one of the victims at the time of their passing, that had appeared to rise from the ground where the DVDs immortalizing their deaths had been buried, almost as though they had been captured within and released at the moment the sun reached down the chute and the rumbling in the earth reached a crescendo.

The ground here has a high concentration of calcite sand, not to mention the dense crystalline formation directly above the underground structure. You see, calcite has unique optical properties. Basically, a light wave enters a calcite crystal from one side, becomes polarized, and breaks into two different waves.

Visible light fell on the electromagnetic spectrum. Could the polarized light, if the wavelength and intensity were just right, have flipped the orientation of the subtle field generated by the bodies of the children?

"Break it down to its most simplistic components," Preston said. "Look at it like a virus. Johnson picks it up while investigating the kidnappings in Montana. He carries it for thirty-some years until it triggers the killings in Edmonton, where the disease is passed to Cochran. After another long period of dormancy, it manifests again in Lander. Now Grant is carrying it, wherever he might be."

"And it should have been you instead."

Preston nodded.

"But this isn't a virus," Dandridge said. "There's no germ that can cause someone to abandon his life and spend the next thirty years in hiding before popping up out of nowhere to begin killing. And what would be the point anyway?"

"The body ages. To survive, there needs to be a new one. A younger one."

"Some sort of transfer of souls? Are you listening to yourself?"

"What do you think those pictures showed, those lights rising from the children's chests when they died? They were in a dim room. And no video recorder uses a flash."

"You think Cochran knew how to extract their souls from their bodies."

"I think whoever carved the petroglyphs did."

"You realize how crazy that sounds?"

Preston's eyes locked onto his. The agent's only answer was silence.

Dandridge turned away and resumed his pacing. His head ached and his teeth screeched as he ground them. There was a surreal logic to Preston's theory that was impossible to ignore, however, the rational part of him insisted that there was no way something so strange could happen, not in the real world where men beat their wives, where mothers dumped newborns in Dumpsters, and where demented people simply killed children without even understanding why themselves.

"What if I'm right?" Preston whispered.

Dandridge stood at the sink and stared out over the unkempt back yard and the decaying swing set, where once there must have been laughter and life. He imagined his daughter's bedroom, the shrine it would become. No one would touch her belongings.

Maggie's stuffed animals would collect dust. Her bed would remain unmade. The clothes on the floor would never be picked up or washed. They would leave her door closed to contain her scent and only open it when they needed to smell her, to feel close to her, to remember her when their memories began to fade.

"What if the man who killed our little girls is still out there?"

Dandridge wiped the tears from his eyes and bit his lip. He thought long and hard before turning back to face Preston, a man to whom he would be bound by pain for the rest of his life. A measure of calmness descended upon him, bringing with it a sense of purpose. His eyes sought Preston's and he finally spoke.

"Then we need to find him."

V

Laramie, Wyoming

Light glowed behind the windows of only two of the houses on the block, both of them toward the end of the street, when Preston pulled to the curb behind the Sheriff's Blazer. No silhouettes appeared in either as they passed. No one walked the street. The moon hid behind a bank of clouds promising early morning rain, its light barely staining them gray. Darkness clung to the front of the bungalow, a shadowed face under the cowl of the roof.

A gentle breeze rustled his hair as he climbed out of the car and quietly eased the door shut behind him. Somewhere in the distance, a barking dog was answered by another. He met the Sheriff on the walkway leading to the front porch, and watched the desolate street while Dandridge picked the lock. They entered the living room and closed the door behind them before flicking on their flashlights.

There had to be something here, something the Sheriff hadn't noticed in his hurry the first time he entered Dr. Grant's home. Or at least they hoped. They wouldn't have another opportunity. Once the university realized Grant wasn't coming back, his belongings would be cleared out to make room for another professor, and they needed to inspect it in exactly the condition Grant had left it.

The authorities were no longer actively seeking the professor. While Dandridge had been able to instigate an APB initially without evidence of a crime, it had been called off in short measure. Risking one's health by sneaking out of the hospital AMA didn't warrant police intervention, and both he and the Sheriff knew they had about as much chance of selling their theory to any law enforcement agency as they would selling audio books to the deaf.

They needed to discover a clue that would lead them to the professor's whereabouts right now or, if the pattern held true, he might not reappear until they were old men themselves. Fortunately, Grant had been in his late forties, and if Preston was correct in his assertion that the whole point of the murders was to secure a younger, more functional body, then they probably wouldn't have to wait the full thirty-some years. Of course, Preston would undoubtedly lose his patience and his mind well before then anyway, even if he managed to live that long with a broken heart and only his rage and obsession pumping through his veins.

The poorly ventilated room had absorbed the meaty scent of the blood crusted in the clothes on the floor, the pockets of which yielded nothing. They tossed the couch cushions and every drawer, searched the mantle, and shook out every book on the shelves. Neither knew exactly what they were looking for. They prayed they would recognize it when they found it. Maybe they could ascertain the climate the professor expected to encounter based on the clothes they could he assume he packed from those he left behind. Perhaps there was a record of how much money had been in the floor safe, or if there had even been any money at all. Bank statements that listed withdrawals could prove useful. The deeds to out-of-state property. A hurriedly scribbled note with an airline flight or bus number, or the residua on the page below the one upon which it had originally been written.

Anything.

Anything at all.

They both knew they were counting on a miracle, but what else did they have to go on? Without a warrant, they couldn't obtain the surveillance camera footage from the bus depots or airports, which weren't about to let them kick back and view the recordings at their leisure, and their unofficial interviews of the employees had yielded only a handful who might have seen a man fitting Grant's description, but none of them could recall where he might have been heading. Several of their statements had even proven contradictory. Grant couldn't have been in two places at once, could he?

The living room gave up no secrets and the entryway closet revealed only a single bare hanger, which they concluded had once held a winter jacket since those that remained were all lightweight.

Dandridge tore apart the master bedroom while Preston worked on the study. No files had been saved onto the hard drive of the desktop computer since before Grant found the medicine wheel and none of the emails in the inbox had been opened after the one that contained the pictures that had sent Grant into the mountains above Lander. When Preston read it, he heard the old man's voice in his mind and imagined the words spoken through that awful smile. He wondered if even now it was affixed to the professor's face, if he was having a good laugh at their expense, which only served to amplify his frustration.

There was nothing here. Searching the house was a fool's errand, but it was all they had. He understood the danger of hope all too well, that it was a scalpel that could be used to keep a man alive or be driven straight through his heart.

The desk drawers produced nothing of consequence, the lone closet even less. There were academic texts and various monographs with a few hardcover novels between, stacks of journals and yellowed newspapers, and a shoebox full of photographs of Grant with a woman who must have once meant something to him. Preston pocketed a stack in hopes of tracking down the reasonably attractive brunette, or at least so that he could have some pictures of the professor to show to potential witnesses. An accordion file contained all of Grant's bills and statements. His 403B suggested Grant would be working long past retirement age, and he never appeared to carry a balance of more than a couple grand in his savings account at any given time. A quick survey led Preston to believe that the professor could have been socking away a decent amount of cash. With the rate the banks and the stock market were failing, it made sense. Better to have no return on his money than to lose it.

He heard footsteps in the hallway and set the file aside. When they were done here, he would take the file folder and the computer tower with him. He didn't figure the professor would return and report them missing.

Dandridge met him outside the door and confirmed his findings with a shake of his head. The expression of futility on his face matched how Preston felt. The Sheriff inclined his head back in the direction from which they had come to signify his intention to search the kitchen. Preston nodded and slipped across the hall into the bathroom. He figured it would take all of about thirty seconds to clear it.

There was nothing but a proliferation of mildew in the shower, nothing hidden in the tank of the toilet, the bowl of which smelled badly of ammonia. Apparently Grant had been blessed with a few spare moments to tend to his bladder before he split.

Preston opened the medicine cabinet and wasn't surprised in the least to find the toothbrush and toothpaste still there. Cochran's hideous smile was proof enough that oral hygiene wasn't a priority. Grant had left behind his deodorant and cologne, his razor and shaving cream, and a fairly broad spectrum of lotions. At least wherever he was now, Grant's dry skin had to be giving him some serious grief.

Bottles of over-the-counter and prescription drugs lined the top shelf. Advil, Tylenol, Motrin. The man must have been prone to headaches. The first bottle was labeled *methylprednisone,* and looked as though it contained a small vial of fluid. There were several more in labeled boxes with trade names Preston didn't recognize: Avonex, Betaseron, and Copasone.

Preston held them in his palm one at a time. They each contained several single-use syringes. That was an awful lot of prescription medication for one man. He didn't think he had much more than expired antibiotics in his cabinet. He studied the labels carefully. Intramuscular injection, once a week. Subcutaneous, daily and every other day. All of them still had several available refills.

He closed his eyes and thought for a long moment, then gathered the prescriptions, headed back across the hall, and sat in front of the computer. Opening a search engine, he typed the drug names in one at a time and quickly scanned the first matching articles. *Methylprednisone* was a corticosteroid that needed to be administered by a health care professional. It was used to alleviate pain in joints. Maybe that explained the OTCs, as well. The Avonex and Betaseron were beta interferons. And all of them combined pointed to the treatment of one specific malady.

Preston called for Dandridge and typed the name of the disease into the search engine. He knew of it, but very little about the specifics. It was an autoimmune disease that attacked the central nervous system, resulting in demyelination, which meant that the axons in the neural pathways could no longer effectively pass signals. It affected the ability of the nerve cells in the brain to communicate with the spinal cord and could possibly cause permanent neurological deficit and loss of conscious muscle control. There was no cure, only treatments designed to prevent acute attacks and ease the suffering after them. But without pharmaceutical intervention, attacks would leave the subject crippled...or worse.

They had finally caught a break.

Dandridge entered the study and leaned over his shoulder.

"Multiple sclerosis?" the Sheriff asked, reading the header. "I don't get it."

Preston held up the pile of prescriptions.

Slowly, a smile spread across Dandridge's face.

"Think he knows?" the Sheriff asked.

"If he doesn't yet, he will soon."

"And if he sees a doctor and tries to get those prescriptions filled..."

"We'll find out."

"And if he doesn't?"

"Then his timetable will be drastically accelerated. Either way, he picked a lemon and he's going to want to get himself into a new vehicle as soon as he realizes it."

"He's going to start taking children again."

Their eyes met and they shared the truth neither could bear to vocalize.

More children were going to die.

"But that will lead us to him," Preston whispered. "From there, we just need to make sure he's never able to do it again."

"And this time, we'll leave no doubt."

Epilogue

Three Years Later

I

June 21ˢᵗ

27 Miles West of Helena, Montana

Preston crouched at the base of a pine trunk in the heart of a cluster of scrub oak, stroking the soft flank of his German shepherd, Wylie, to keep him from whining. He fished a milk bone out of his pocket every few minutes to calm the excited dog. The sun beat down on the forest, drying the detritus to the point that a single errant match could blacken half the state. He couldn't quite see the bottom of the ravine through the dense grove of firs, but he had a good idea of what awaited them down there. What looked like ribbons of heat rising from the ground made the forest shimmer. His free hand caressed the Beretta in his shoulder holster. He prayed that once Dandridge was in position and they were ready to roll, he would have the opportunity to use it.

"Good boy," he whispered.

The whipping wind stole the words from his lips.

Any moment now, a crackle of static on his walkie-talkie would signal Dandridge's readiness. The last nine years of Preston's life had been building up to this moment. He couldn't wait for it to be over.

Sixteen months ago, on February 18ᵗʰ, an indigent had been treated at St. Peter's Hospital in Helena, Montana for an acute attack of what the triage nurse in the emergency room termed "MS-like symptoms." He had simply wandered in off the street in the middle of the night and split before the tab could be settled. There had been thirty-six similar cases over the preceding three years across the Western United States and Canada. Preston and Dandridge had investigated each and every one of them. Unofficially, anyway. But it wasn't until the former Sheriff showed the charge nurse in the ER at St. Peter's one of the pictures of Grant that they knew they had finally found him. The vagrant had registered under a false name and the address he had listed proved non-existent. There had been little of any real value to go on, but at least they had pinned him down geographically.

Confirmation came thirty days later on March 21st when Kyle and Liza Covington reported the abduction of their ten year-old son Craig to the Boulder Police. Preston had followed the investigation through his channels at the FBI and built a case file from afar. Three months later, on June 19th, he added Rachael Sutter, who was taken in broad daylight from the park across the street from her house in Townsend. By the time nine year-old Victoria Timonson went missing on her way home from school on September 20th, Preston had transferred to the small Helena Field Office. When Jennifer Metcalf was abducted four days before Christmas from her backyard a mere fifteen miles away, he was the first on the scene, barely beating Officer Keith Dandridge of the Helena Police Department.

The Sheriff of a county in which twenty-eight children were found heinously murdered generally didn't fare well at re-election time, but that hadn't mattered to Dandridge, who hadn't had the desire to run again anyway. Not after returning home at the end of his shift one day to find his dead wife on their bed, still clutching the bottle of Sominex she had downed to usher herself into a permanent sleep. Like Preston, Dandridge said he kept the house to remind him of what should have been, even if subconsciously he knew the real reason was that one day he would return there with the intention of rejoining his family in the ever-after. He was overqualified for the job of a beat cop, but the force had been happy to welcome him aboard, and he had been even happier to gain access to their considerable resources, most notably the surveillance equipment with which he became intimately acquainted during whatever free time he could spare. The rest was spent surveying the 976,000 acres of Helena National Forest, which sat at the epicenter of the abductions, with Preston and the German shepherd he had purchased and trained to track specific scents. Among them, the smell of the tattered bed linens they had removed from Grant's house.

The onset of winter and the feet of snow that accumulated in the Big Belt Mountains allowed them to narrow their search parameters. After all, a man might be able to hide in those woods forever, but there were only so many places where he would be able to survive when the temperature plummeted below zero for days at a time and the frequent snowstorms prohibited travel, yet he had still eluded them.

Volunteers had tromped through the forest following the last two kidnappings, but had found no sign of either child. Neither search had lasted very long as they had encountered nothing of significance. No sign of fresh tracks off the beaten paths, shreds of clothing, or, God forbid, human remains. The searches had been instigated out of futility more than anything else. There had been no signs to indicate the children had been taken anywhere near the forest. The community had simply felt the need to do something productive instead of sitting on its collective hands waiting for the bodies to be found in a Dumpster somewhere, or worse still, never found at all. Only Preston and Dandridge had known that somewhere out there in those steep valleys, under the shadows of the sheer, icy peaks, was a man who had already killed the children and intended to use what was left of them to make his escape from a body that by now had to be rapidly failing him.

The walkie-talkie under Preston's jacket hissed with static, a brief burst that barely stood apart from the wind. He looked for Dandridge through the overlapping branches, which shifted and changed directions with the unpredictable gusts, but couldn't even see the bottom of the hill in front of him, let alone the rise on the other side. He had to trust that the partner fate had thrust upon him was preparing to break cover and begin his approach.

He tied Wylie's leash around the tree trunk and scattered the remainder of the biscuits onto the dirt, hoping the distraction would prevent the dog from barking and betraying their presence. Raising his pistol, he crawled through the brush and started down the slope through knee-high wild grasses, keeping the thick forest between him and their ultimate goal.

The Division of Wildlife had provided they break they needed. One of their tagged black bears had been dumped in a campground at the edge of the National Forest, its right front paw mangled from a trap. The anterior aspect of its throat had been slit so deeply it barely remained attached to the body. The wound had been inflicted postmortem, presumably after the bear had already bled out. Its movements prior to its death had been tracked by satellite and its last known location marked about eight miles up Thompson Canyon on the southern slope of Mt. Vance. Dandridge had taken the call from the Park Ranger and begun an investigation he expected to lead him nowhere. After all, it was a bear, not a person, and the poachers in the area were rarely caught. If the men who stalked dangerous game like bears knew one thing, it was how to cover their tracks. Dandridge had gone through the motions regardless, and even studied the satellite images charting the bear's range with the Ranger, who had said, innocuously enough, "We think he had a den in one of those caves up there on Vance. There are a ton of them through there. All sorts of strange natural formations out there by Crook's Grove."

"Crook's Grove?" Dandridge had asked.

"That's just what we DOW guys call it. Nothing official or anything like that. It's just got these weird trees that grow like corkscrews. You know...crooked?"

Mere minutes earlier, a young girl named Jerica Moore was abducted from the playground of Jefferson Elementary School. The teacher's aides had searched the surrounding neighborhood and every nook and cranny in the building while the principal attempted to contact her parents at work. He finally reached her father an hour later. Douglas Moore confirmed that neither he nor the child's mother had picked her up, and notified the police himself. When the call finally went out, Preston and Dandridge were already on their way up the winding washboard road toward the grove the Ranger had mentioned.

Four hours later, as the midday sun approached its zenith, they had crested a ridge and glimpsed the stony face of Mt. Vance. Wylie had fought against his leash, attracted by a strong scent that matched the strip of fabric in the plastic bag in Preston's pocket. They had studied the topographical and satellite maps on the way, and had a good idea of what to expect. The forest grew up against the steep granite slope at the base of a bowl eroded by seasonal runoff. There was a stream several hundred yards downhill. No trails led to their position, only an almost magnetic pull that drew them across interminable fields and under the lush canopy, over steep ridges and down stone-studded embankments.

And now, they converged at the edge of the uneven copse of twisted firs and stared in the direction of the mountain. An occasional scuffing sound broke the silence unmarred by birdsong. They kept the wind in their faces so as not to betray their scent or the sound of their footfalls. Preston adjusted his grip on his pistol until it felt just right, and raised his stare to meet Dandridge's. The gravity of the moment hung between them. Everything they had ever done had led them to this point. The past and future blended into the moment. This was where both their old and new lives ended.

"You remember our deal?" Dandridge whispered.

Their eyes locked for a long moment.

Preston finally nodded, and together they struck off toward the granite cliff, an occasional gray blur through the branches above them. The trees thinned significantly ahead, creating gaps through which they could easily be seen. They clung to the trunks, staying low to the ground, moving slowly, cautiously, so as not to make even a single twig snap. He listened for a child's cry, but heard only the wail of the wind. Deep down, he knew better than to hope that the little girl was still alive. She'd been dead the moment Grant took her.

He crinkled his nose as they neared a small clearing in the center of the grove. A glance at Dandridge confirmed that he had smelled it as well. His sense of relief that they had found Grant after all this time was dampened by the implication of the stench.

They had found the missing children.

II

Dandridge pulled his undershirt up over his mouth and nose. He not only smelled, but tasted, a scent he remembered far too clearly. The foul stench of decomposition. Just like before. The rotten smell of the inside of something that hadn't been designed to be opened. Tears rolled from the corners of his eyes, stinging his wind-abraded cheeks. He hated himself for what he'd allowed to happen to his daughter, and for what he'd been forced to allow to happen to the children after her in order to track the monster to his lair.

It all ended right here. Right now. This he vowed. Even if it cost him his life, Grant was not leaving this forest.

A shuffling sound from ahead.

A shadow passed across the ground between a pair of twisted trunks about ten yards away.

He glanced at Preston and nodded to his left. The agent darted away from him and ducked behind a clump of shrubs, while he dashed to his right and hid behind a gnarled fir. Before they could burst into the clearing, they needed to establish what they were up against. They needed to evaluate every possible scenario, to anticipate Grant's strategy, to determine whether or not they were stumbling into a trap. And most importantly, they needed to establish if the girl was still alive, even though both of them understood on a primal level that she was already dead.

Dandridge eased around the side of the trunk and risked a quick peek. A small ring of stones, perhaps fifteen feet in diameter. Twenty-eight spokes radiating outward from a rusted iron post. A miniature recreation of the medicine wheel near Lander. Shadows danced on the ground, elongated by the solstice sun, which reached through the shifting gaps overhead. He looked up at their source. Bodies. Five children suspended from hooks driven into the thick branches of the lower canopy. Hung like slabs of meat. Wired together in a circle. On the ground, a circle of electric fence, identifiable by the plastic clips holding the wires, powered by a series of batteries in square plastic housings. A rusted length of iron was planted in the center. Near the perimeter, six tiny mounds of darker soil.

Dandridge caught a flash of movement and ducked back.

Grant limped from around the far side of the clearing to his right toward the center of the medicine wheel. He struggled with the weight of something heavy draped over his shoulder like a roll of old carpet. His legs were visibly deformed, bent backward just below his knees. He walked with a staggering gait and grunted with each step. The sunlight momentarily caught his face and illuminated not the awful smile that haunted Dandridge's dreams, but bared teeth and deep creases around his eyes, an expression of great pain. The professor turned his back to them and hefted his cargo up from his shoulder with a groan. He raised the naked girl by her armpits, aligned her with the last available hook in the ring, and shoved her back against it with the sound of snapping ribs. He stepped back, appraised his work, and gave the girl's ankles a sharp tug to make sure she was properly seated. Blood rolled down her torso and spiraled around her legs from the laceration across her throat, which was nearly hidden by her lolling head and the locks of dark hair hanging over her chest. The droplets shimmered as they dripped from her toes and pattered the forest floor with an arrhythmic tapping noise.

Dandridge looked toward Preston. Their eyes met. He saw the expression of resignation on the agent's face. They were too late to save the girl, but there would not be another. There would never be another.

Preston gave the nod and they swung out from behind the trees, pistols raised.

Grant still faced the opposite direction. His posture stiffened. Slowly, his right hand sought the pocket of his filthy jacket.

"Don't move!" Preston shouted, his words reverberating through the valley. "Hands where I can see them!"

"I figured the bear would do the trick," Grant said. His voice was different. He sounded old, beaten, pained. But there was something else, something that made Dandridge's skin crawl.

"Can't even leave wild animals to their own devices anymore, can we? Have to control them like everything else in this pathetic world."

Grant's hand paused near his pocket. After a moment, it resumed its movement.

Dandridge aimed his weapon and fired.

Grant's elbow exploded in a cloud of blood and bone fragments. He howled beneath the echoing thunder of the report and fell to his knees, cradling his nearly severed forearm to his chest. Slowly, he scooted away from them and reached for something on the ground in front of him. There was a click and the hum of an electrical current.

The ground trembled subtly.

Preston's weapon discharged to his left with a deafening blast. A scorched hole appeared in the shoulder of Grant's jacket as an arc of blood slapped across the ground in front of him. The impact tossed the professor forward onto his chest.

There was an electrical snap and Grant's body convulsed. He rolled inside the circle and onto his back on a short row of stones.

Dandridge crossed the clearing, stepped over the wire and ducked around the lifeless legs suspended from above, their feet livid with settled blood, and stood over Grant, who merely stared back up at him through dead eyes that radiated a palpable coldness.

Preston walked up beside him, his shadow falling over Grant.

"I've done nothing but think about this moment for nearly a decade," Preston said, leveling the barrel of the pistol between Grant's eyes. "I only wish I could make this last longer."

Dandridge felt the same way. He had built up this confrontation in his mind to the point that it felt like the culmination of his entire life. No matter what they did to this man, it would never be enough. There was no physical way of inflicting enough pain to compensate for the loss of his daughter, for the horrors she had endured at the end of her far-too-short life. He wanted to violate this man in a way that would send shivers of agony through his very soul.

But no matter what he did, there would be no healing his broken heart. This man had cost him everything he loved in this world, everything that made life worth living. And still, there was one thing he needed to know.

"What are you?" Dandridge whispered.

Grant looked up at him, his face crumpled by pain, distorted by the rippling air between them, and in his eyes Dandridge read his answer.

The professor laughed, a horrible, gut-wrenching sound that echoed through the wilderness like the cries of dying children.

III

The air wavered around Preston and the ground shuddered. He trained his pistol on Grant's forehead. All around him, bright points of light rose from the freshly turned sections of earth, the same optical illusions he remembered from before. Slowly, they began to swirl beneath where the bodies hung. This time there were fewer of them, six in total, one for each of the children. Their captured souls, Preston now understood, only now being set free from their imprisonment on the recordings of their deaths.

Grant's laugh died with a choked sob. Preston saw a momentary expression of terror cross his face. His eyes widened with fear.

A concussive blast from his right and the professor's forehead imploded, spraying blood across the stone design and the dirt. His jaws worked up and down a moment longer. His legs scraped at the ground. Slower and slower, until finally they stopped.

Preston turned toward Dandridge, who still held the smoldering pistol in front of him. A twirl of smoke drifted from the barrel. The spent casing glinted off to his right.

The small lights winked out of existence.

Dandridge lowered his pistol to his side and stared down at Grant's body for a long moment. He finally shook his head as if to break the trance that held him and kicked one of the battery packs across the clearing, killing the electrical current with a crackle.

The movement around them ceased. The air, the ground, the entire forest became still.

"It's over," Dandridge said, and turned away from the corpse.

"Yeah," Preston whispered. "It's finally over."

Together, they headed back in the direction from which they had come. Preston took the lead and ascended the slope toward where he could barely see Wylie struggling against his tether through the shrub. There was still much to be done. There would be questions to be answered, statements to be made, and most importantly, there were the remains of the children to return to their parents for proper burial. He hated to think about the pain they were about to endure.

But there was still one more thing he needed to do first.

Wylie barked as they approached. He rose to his full height to gain leverage and tugged against his leash.

"So what are you going to do now?" Preston asked.

"I don't know." Preston heard the crackle of Dandridge's tread on the detritus behind him. "I still can't believe he's really dead. I think I'm going to need some time for it to sink in, to see if there's even anything left for me out there."

Preston nodded.

Wylie dropped to all fours, lowered his head, and pricked his ears. The coarse fur on his haunches rose. He released a growl through bared teeth.

"I'd be surprised if there's anything left for either of us," Preston said. The footsteps stopped behind him, but he continued to walk. "You remember our deal?"

"Yeah. I remember."

Again, Preston nodded. He readjusted his grip on his weapon, and in one swift motion, spun around, raised his pistol, and fired.

In that split-second, he saw surprise register on Dandridge's face. His gun had been trained on Preston's back.

Blood burst from the right side of Dandridge's upper chest as he toppled backward. He managed to squeeze off a shot that careened harmlessly into the forest before his heels caught in the grass and sent him sprawling to the ground.

Wylie continued to growl.

Preston walked toward Dandridge, kicked the gun away from his hand, and stared down at him for several seconds.

Dandridge sputtered blood and tried to sit up.

Preston shot him below the opposite clavicle. The upper lobes of his lungs punctured, they would slowly fill with blood until he could no longer breathe.

"The deal was we save the kill shot until after we make him suffer," Preston said. He turned his back on the man, whose heels dug into the dirt in an effort to push him toward his pistol. Preston heard the scraping sounds and the wet, rasping inhalations as he returned to the tree where he had tied his dog. He ruffled the fur on the dog's head and whispered, "Good boy."

He leaned around the trunk and grabbed the handle of the hatchet he had hidden there when they arrived.

"You see," Preston said as he tromped through the scrub oak and walked downhill toward Dandridge, "if you were actually Dandridge, you would have known that."

The man tried to speak, but only ended up coughing out a mouthful of blood that ran down his cheeks and around his ears.

Preston stood over him, watching him kick at the earth, moving in increments of inches. He held up the hatchet so the man could get a good look at it, so he could clearly comprehend what was about to happen. Preston wanted to see the expression of fear on Dandridge's borrowed face when he did.

The man raised a trembling hand and gurgled what Preston hoped was a nasty epithet.

Preston raised the hatchet and swung it down on Dandridge's right ankle. The blood rushed out from the wound. It took another chop to sever the foot.

He studied the man's face, the pinched eyes and bared teeth of his former friend, and tried to memorize it for both of them. Dandridge would soon be with his family again. Preston firmly believed that. He had no choice but to, as one day he hoped to be reunited with his.

"Her name was Savannah Marie Preston." He raised the hatchet and brought it down on the opposite ankle with a *crack*. "She was ten years old." Again, the blade whistled through the air and relieved the man of his opposite foot. "And I loved her more than anything in the world."

The fires of hell burned behind Dandridge's eyes, windows through which Preston could see a fathomless past filled with the infliction of unlimited pain. An eternity of suffering as ancient as the ground upon which he now stood. A parasitic consciousness of pure evil that until this very moment had never known fear.

He stepped on Dandridge's forearm to hold the wrist in place.

The sound of breaking bones echoed through the forest well into the afternoon.

The shadows of the twisted firs grew longer.

Eventually, the sound of distant sirens reached the valley.

And somewhere behind the rocky peaks of the Big Belt Range, the sun finally set on the longest day of the year.

How Full of Crap Am I?

During the process of researching this novel, I encountered a ton of interesting facts that I incorporated into the story. If I couldn't find the necessary science to make a certain scene work, I made it up. This is a work of fiction, after all. Now that you've read *Innocents Lost*, it's time to see if you, dear reader, could tell the difference. So, let's play a little game called "How Full of Crap Am I?" I hope some of the answers surprise you.

Do decomposing corpses really generate electromagnetic fields?

According to a theory put forth by researchers at the Oak Ridge National Laboratory they do! This phenomenon has been demonstrated by divining rods similar those used by dowsers, although made of angled metal wires rather than forked, green sticks. The wires twitch when in the proximity of rotting remains. Scientists speculate that chemical changes in the body transform it into a kind of battery capable of producing a quantifiable electromagnetic charge. Keep that little tidbit in mind next time you read a zombie book.

This is actually the premise upon which the entire book was constructed. I first encountered the concept in *Carved in Bone* by Jefferson Bass a few years ago, and I thought it was so cool that I knew I had to use it at some point, so I set it aside and let it percolate in my head until the right idea for a story formed around it. I wondered if there was a way to harness that energy, and if so, even theoretically, what could one possibly hope to do with it? Going "green" by using bodies as an alternative fuel source like some freakish version of Ed Begley Jr. didn't sound nearly as fun as utilizing them to achieve immortality.

Are glories real?

Indubitably. A glory is an optical phenomenon caused by the backscattering of light from a cloud or mist of uniformly-sized water droplets. In China, it's called Buddha's Light. You'll often see glories in photographs taken from sea- and aircrafts. In *Innocents Lost*, however, there was no mist in the clearing with the medicine wheel. So while glories may be real, I cheated in the story to rationalize the physical manifestation of the children's souls. In this case, I say I'm only half full of crap.

Do medicine wheels really exist and can they really chart the solstice?

Of course they exist, as I'm sure you already know. The majority of you are undoubtedly much smarter than I am. Also known as sacred hoops, there are more than seventy in Alberta alone. Arguably the most impressive example is the Bighorn Medicine Wheel in Wyoming, the one upon which my fictional wheel is based. They were constructed to act as solar calendars that tracked the rising and setting of the moon, sun, and stars exactly as detailed in this novel. One medicine wheel was even dated to more than 4,500 years old, the same age as its more notorious cousin of similar function, Stonehenge. (That's 2500 B.C.E. for those of you keeping score, 4,107 years before the first permanent English settlement at Jamestown.) Archeologists theorize that subsequent generations of Plains Indians continued to add to the original structure, changing its function and meaning over time. And while they do accurately chart the solstice, no one will ever know their original purpose. Why were they built in the first place? What happened on this one day each year that needed to be marked? That's the mystery, and where the medicine wheel becomes integral to the story. We'll address my usage of it next, but as far as the medicine wheel itself, mine is historically consistent, if on a slightly more elaborate scale. So in this instance, I'm far from full of crap.

I knew when I was plotting this novel that I wanted a supernatural element to the kidnappings and ultimate deaths of the children, but I needed there to be a scientific foundation to explain the possibility of soul-transfer. I couldn't live with the idea of a soul just up and leaving a failing vessel in search of a new one, so I probably spent as much time transforming the medicine wheel into a weak particle accelerator, with the energy differential between the rings of electrical current both below and above, and the influence of gravitational forces, as I did writing the novel. For those of you who've been with me from the start (and I thank you sincerely for it, if you have), you may have noticed the similarities to my novelette *Zero*. If so, you're paying better attention than I am. I didn't until I was writing this.

Is there a real petroglyph depicting the soul-transfer rite described in this book?

Alas, no. This is where I'm totally full of crap. To the best of my knowledge, there is no carving that could serve as a blueprint for soul-transfer. I'm sure my wife would appreciate me coaxing someone like Brad Pitt out into the woods for a quick switch, but I digress. I will say that all of the elements I used to create my fictional petroglyph were accurate, if a hodgepodge of styles borrowed from various Plains Indian tribes. The swirls, the human shapes, the stars, the sun. The two-dimensional representation of three-dimensional objects. I was faithful to the original style and meaning of these symbols in my execution. And the location where it was found is real. You could visit this strange rock covered with etchings several thousands of years old, you just won't find mine among them.

My fictional petroglyph was fashioned after the Hopi "end of the world" prophecy on Prophecy Rock, near Oraibi, Arizona, which depicts "life paths" connecting larger and smaller figures and wavy lines of ascent. The majority of the elements I inserted around this basic framework I owe primarily to the Anasazi and Sioux. I had a lot of fun at this stage. I hope it read well, and that you had a little bit of fun with it, as well.

Are the statistics regarding missing children accurate?

In this case, I wish more than anything I were full of crap. All of the statistics regarding missing children and child abduction are accurate, and borrowed faithfully from the National Center for Missing & Exploited Children. None of them were altered in any form or fashion. I hope you were every bit as surprised and shocked by them as I was. Do you want to know what's worse? This problem is exponentially worse in the United States than in any other nation in the world. Not just a little bit worse. A lot worse. Exponentially. Meaning worse by factors of ten. This is almost exclusively an American problem. An American disease. Like serial killers, we breed pedophiles and monsters. The most civilized nation in the world, the global leader in commerce and industry, has no regard for its most important natural resource: its children. They're treated like every other natural resource, exploited, abused, and then discarded. Perhaps you find my stance a little on the emotional side. Well, you're right. This, to me, is an indication that as a people, as a species, we're doomed. If not, we should be.

I'm not the touchy-feely liberal type. I believe that unless you're willing to do whatever it takes to win a war, permanently, there's no point in fighting one. Registering sex offenders is a step in the right direction, but it's not a solution. What Freddy Krueger's neighbors did to him? That was a solution. Anyone convicted of abusing a child, or worse, should be subjected to a punishment more commensurate to the crime. Confining them in a facility with other sexual degenerates may, on the surface, sound amusing, but in no way can this be considered rehabilitation. It's just fueling the fire. And then we turn them loose again on the streets with a whole new bag of tricks. I say we sever the nerve tracts controlling their arms and legs and make it so they can never manhandle anyone ever again. Perhaps I am getting a little more liberal in my old age.

When I first starting writing *Innocents Lost*, my daughter was eleven years old, the most common age and gender for abduction. I tried to make Savannah the same age, but I just couldn't do it. It cut too close to the bone. Making her ten may sound like an inconsequential alteration, but it was necessary. It's the first time I've truly shied away from anything in my work. The course of the novel was predicated upon the actions of a grieving father. In order for the novel to flow, I had to be Phil Preston while I was writing him, which, at times, I found almost painful. What would I do in his shoes? If my daughter were missing, how would I react in this situation? There were times when I simply didn't want to be Preston anymore. I didn't want his life. And hopefully that helped make him more believable. Of all of the characters I've written, he's the most like the real "me." For better or worse.

Do energy vortices exist and are they really strong enough to cause aberrant tree growth?

There is no more evidence to prove the existence of energy vortices than there is to prove the existence of God, but that doesn't change the fact that people believe in both. An energy vortex has been described as a cyclone of spiritual forces, a dust devil of swirling energy. The theory is that energy vortices form at the convergence of energy meridians, or ley lines, to create pockets of electromagnetic energy that contribute to an uplifting and rejuvenating spiritual experience. Many sacred temples, like the Pyramids of Giza, are supposedly built on such sites. Here in America, our most famous energy vortices are near Sedona, Arizona (I found this odd fact while researching *Bloodletting*), where they are inexplicably pluralized as vortexes. Every year, thousands of Birkenstock-wearing, crystal-toting, mystically sensitive people make a pilgrimage to the red Sedona desert to recharge their spiritual batteries. And while no tests have been able to conclusively demonstrate electromagnetic activity of any kind, tourists continue to erect cairns (saw that one coming, didn't you?) at the epicenter of these "vortexes". The only physical evidence that any kind of invisible force is at work in the vicinity is the large number of juniper trees whose trunks have grown in twisting, corkscrew configurations, even in the midst of normal specimens.

On this subject, I bow to your judgment. If you believe in these vortices, then I am minimally full of crap. If, however, you find them to be New Age mumbo-jumbo, then I suppose I'll just have to live with your condemnation.

MICHAEL McBRIDE

is the bestselling author of *Ancient Enemy*, *Bloodletting*, *Burial Ground*, *Fearful Symmetry*, *Predatory Instinct*, *Sunblind*, *The Coyote*, and *Vector Borne*. His novella *Snowblind* won the 2012 DarkFuse Readers Choice Award and received honorable mention in *The Best Horror of the Year*. He lives in Avalanche Territory with his wife and kids.

To explore the author's other works, please visit
www.michaelmcbride.net.

Made in the USA
Coppell, TX
05 February 2022

72978597R00132